Once again, [...] rescue as he [...] around her.

She inhaled his comforting scent, not expensive cologne, but pure, potent masculinity. The smell made her feel safe and protected...and incredibly aroused.

She wanted to go home with him. She'd wanted to know what it felt like for this man to take control of her body the way he'd taken control of her mind and actions for the past five hours. She'd done things that would have been unthinkable for her only hours ago. Would Nick have the same effect on her in bed?

"I'm sorry." He stroked her hair. "You're not safe here."

But how safe would she be with him...in his home, in his bed?

CAROL ERICSON

A DOCTOR-NURSE ENCOUNTER

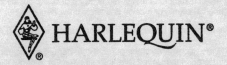

TORONTO • NEW YORK • LONDON
AMSTERDAM • PARIS • SYDNEY • HAMBURG
STOCKHOLM • ATHENS • TOKYO • MILAN • MADRID
PRAGUE • WARSAW • BUDAPEST • AUCKLAND

For my sister, Janice.

ISBN-13: 978-0-373-69346-7
ISBN-10:   0-373-69346-X

A DOCTOR-NURSE ENCOUNTER

ABOUT THE AUTHOR

Carol Ericson lives with her husband and two sons in Southern California, home of state-of-the-art cosmetic surgery, wild freeway chases, palm trees bending in the Santa Ana winds, and a million amazing stories. These stories, along with hordes of virile men and feisty women, clamor for release from Carol's head. It makes for some interesting headaches until she sets them free to fulfill their destinies and her readers' fantasies. To find out more about Carol, her books and her strange headaches, please visit her Web site at www.carolericson.com, "where romance flirts with danger."

Books by Carol Ericson

HARLEQUIN INTRIGUE
1034—THE STRANGER AND I
1079—A DOCTOR-NURSE ENCOUNTER

CAST OF CHARACTERS

Lacey Kirk—This nurse runs a doctor's office with smooth efficiency, but her world is turned upside down when that doctor is murdered. Now she must depend on the secretive Dr. Marino for protection even as she risks her heart.

Dr. Nick Marino—He keeps secrets to shield his family from danger. His encounter with Lacey, a feisty nurse who demands answers, strips away his protective layers. Will Lacey still want the man she discovers beneath?

Dr. Joseph Buonfoglio—The grumpy doctor has secrets of his own, and his murder reveals them one by one, putting his employees in danger.

T.J. Paglietti—A small-time hood on the run from the mob. If the De Luca family discovers his identity before he can testify against one of their own, his life is over.

Frankie De Luca—He yearns for respect from his father and revenge for his brother—and he's willing to kill to achieve his goals.

Petra Sorenson—She has a crush on her boss, Dr. Marino, and an insatiable need to prove she can find other men as substitutes. But her latest "substitute" has an ulterior motive.

Abby Buonfoglio—Dr. Buonfoglio's gentle daughter has Down syndrome. Does she also hold the key to her father's murder?

Chapter One

A person could die of asphyxiation down here. Lacey Kirk held her breath against the noxious wave of exhaust fumes that greeted her as she stepped out of the elevator into the parking garage.

The heels of her boots clipped on the cement, creating a lonely echo in the empty lot. Most of the doctors, including her boss, parked on the lower level. At this hour, the cars in the upper levels cleared out quickly, leaving gaping parking stalls in their wake.

She scooped her keys out of her purse, dropping them onto the garage floor, where they skidded underneath her Jetta. She uttered a curse.

"Hope that battery doesn't pop out of the remote again," she commented to no one in particular.

She crouched down and pinched her small desk key between her fingers, dragging the key chain toward her. Damn. She forgot to lock her desk after she pulled out the appointment book to check Dr. B's appointments for tomorrow.

She stood up, sawing her bottom lip with her teeth. Normally, she wouldn't worry about it, but she'd left the front door of the office unlocked for the deli delivery guy. She'd ordered Dr. B a sandwich before leaving for the night. Someone had to take care of the man.

Sighing, she dropped the keys back in her purse and trudged back toward the elevator. At least this would give her a chance to make sure Dr. B got his food.

As she rushed off the elevator, she almost collided with a man carrying an armful of file folders while fiddling with his BlackBerry and holding a cell phone. A few files slipped off the top of the stack and fell to the polished floor.

"Watch where you're going." Dr. Nick Marino's black brows collided over his aquiline nose, and two spots of color stained his broad cheekbones before he stooped to pick up the files.

"You're the one juggling electronic devices. Why don't you watch where you're going?" She dug a fist in her hip and tapped the toe of her pointed boot as the doctor straightened up, clutching the folders in his hand.

He dropped his BlackBerry into the pocket of his white coat, which flapped open, revealing his tailored shirt molded to his chest. Pec implants? His full lips twisted into a semblance of a smile. Did men get collagen treatments?

"I'm sorry. You're right." He patted his pocket. "Multitasking."

She rolled her eyes and pivoted toward the corner.

"Lacey, right? You work for Dr. Joseph Buonfoglio."

"Yeah, Lacey." She glanced over her shoulder. He knew her name? She didn't think she was worthy of Dr. Perfect's notice.

"I've seen you over at San Francisco General. You're in the hospice/palliative nursing program, aren't you?"

She spun around. She'd seen him at SF General, too. Pretty hard to miss a six-foot-two Adonis with groupies trailing him around the hospital. "That's right. I'm in the hospice program. What does an internationally acclaimed cosmetic surgeon, darling of the rich and famous medical-convention rock star know about a hospice?"

He raised an eyebrow just as she stumbled around the corner.

She covered her face with her hands. *Smart move, Lacey.* The hunky Dr. Marino may be arrogant, but he also had connections. She giggled. Even getting kicked out of the hospice program was worth the look on his face. Well, almost.

Stepping up to the office door, she grabbed the doorknob, but it didn't turn. She jiggled it. Had Dr. B locked the door after the food arrived? That didn't seem likely.

She slipped her key into the lock and pushed open the door. Rustling noises echoed in the office, and the door that separated the rooms in the back from the reception area stood open. Dr. B must be eating his sandwich.

She sniffed the air. Cappicola didn't have that heavy, metallic smell. It reminded her of the smell in the hospital... the hospital emergency room. Her heart banged against her rib cage as she crept toward the gaping door.

Placing a hand against the wall, she inched forward. She peered into Dr. B's office and clutched the doorjamb to steady the spinning room.

Dr. B lay crumpled on the floor in front of his desk, a pool of blood soaking into the carpet under his head. The scream that barreled up from her lungs snagged in her throat, and she choked.

A large figure with a black ski mask and black gloves stepped into the hallway from the supply room. His eyes glittered through the holes in the mask, and Lacey stumbled back, banging her elbow against the wall.

The shooting pain released the tightness in her chest and she screamed as she scrambled toward the reception area and the door she'd left open. She felt the man's body heat behind her before he yanked her hair, pulling her backward. He twisted her hair, jerking her head against his body, his garlic-scented breath bathing her cheek.

She stomped on his foot with her high heel. He grunted but tightened his grip, circling her throat with his other arm.

Rather than immobilizing her, the terror raging through her body spurred her to action. Her purse slipped from her shoulder and dangled from her arm. She shook it down farther, gathered the strap in her hand and swung back, but the blow barely grazed her captor's hip.

She jabbed her throbbing elbow into his rib cage and had the satisfaction of hearing his muffled curse. The vise pinioning her neck loosened, and she gathered her breath and let loose with another scream that tore through her ragged throat.

"What the hell?" Dr. Marino charged through the office door, and Lacey took advantage of her assailant's surprise as his hold on her slackened.

She wrenched out of his grasp, tumbling forward onto her hands and knees. She looked back in time to see Nick plant his fist against the man's face. As the intruder staggered back, Nick reached forward and twisted the ski mask so that the eyeholes were no longer positioned over the man's eyes. The man raised his gloved hands to correct his mask, desperate to keep it on, and Nick punched him in the gut.

The man grunted but kicked Nick's midsection, sending him reeling backward and crashing into a table. Magazines scattered and a heavy lamp tipped over, the lampshade bouncing across the carpet.

"Look out. He might have a weapon." Lacey crawled to the door and dumped out her purse, scrambling for her cell phone.

The masked man advanced on Nick, still bent over the table. Nick grabbed the base of the lamp, spun around and brought it down toward the man's head. The blow glanced off the side of the intruder's skull as he brought his arm up to knock the lamp back.

Lacey gripped the phone in her stiff fingers and punched in 911 just as Nick and the intruder fell to the floor next to her. Lacey flattened her body against the floor. Amazingly, the man's ski mask still covered his face.

The 911 operator answered the phone, and Lacey shouted, "Please come right away. Someone's been hurt. The man's still here." Then she gave the operator the address and disconnected.

"Who ordered the—" The deli delivery guy, a skinny teenager, gaped in the doorway, his eyes bulging out of his head as he dropped the food.

Nick paused at the intrusion, and the man reached for the heavy doorstop under the table and swung it at Nick's head.

"Nick!" Lacey screamed and dropped the phone. The doorstop skimmed the side of Nick's head instead of flattening his face as he jerked out of the way.

Nick collapsed, and the man with the ski mask jumped up and shoved the delivery guy out of his way. His foot smashed the bag of food on the floor as he sprinted down the hallway.

"Go after him." Lacey dragged herself up and waved her arms at the teenager frozen against the doorjamb.

"Are you crazy?" He swallowed, his Adam's apple resembling a golf ball. "That guy's huge."

Nick moaned, and Lacey hobbled over on her knees and inspected the gash on the side of his head. She shrugged out of her sweater and yanked her cotton T-shirt over her head. The delivery guy's eyes got bigger and rounder. She folded the T-shirt into a square and pressed it against Nick's wound, staunching the flow of blood.

She glanced over her shoulder at the speechless teenager. "Hold this bandage on his head. I have to check on my boss in the back."

"Th-there's someone else here?"

"Yeah, but he's...unconscious." Tilting her chin toward the door, she said, "Keep an eye out for the emergency response team."

Dr. B was more than unconscious. She didn't want to go back to his office. Judging from the amount of blood on the carpet, she doubted he could use her help now.

She returned to his office, anyway, and tiptoed toward his still form, as if afraid she'd wake him. She pressed a fist to her mouth as her gaze hitched on the gun in Dr. B's slack hand. When did he get a gun? Didn't do him much good today.

She could see now that the intruder, the murderer, had smashed in one side of Dr. B's skull. A marble bookend, smeared with blood and hair, lay next to Dr. B's body. Pressing her fingertips against his neck, she felt for a pulse. No sign of life.

What if she had stayed? Would Dr. B be alive? Would she be dead?

She brushed a tear from her cheek and tripped back to the disordered reception area.

The teen looked up. "How's your boss?"

She shook her head and shooed him away. Leaning over Nick's body, she kept the pressure on the makeshift bandage. She inhaled the incongruous aroma of spicy cologne and antiseptic wash.

His spiky, dark lashes stirred, and she murmured, "Dr. Perfect doesn't look so perfect now."

NICK'S BODY ACHED ALL OVER, especially on the left side of his head, right above his ear where a lead weight pressed against his skull.

He opened one eye. A pair of shapely breasts molded by a

white, lacy bra hovered above him. Had to be natural. He opened the other eye. A lock of silky, dark hair tickled his chest. Had he died and gone to heaven?

He dragged his gaze away from the alluring sight in front of him, where it collided with a pair of stormy green eyes. He'd seen those eyes shooting angry sparks earlier, before all the chaos.

Lacey. Lacey from Dr. Buonfoglio's office. Lacey, the aspiring hospice nurse. Lacey, the master of torture.

He shifted and wrapped his fingers around her deceptively delicate wrist. "I think that's enough pressure. I'm in danger of losing oxygen to my brain."

She sucked in a breath as he heard someone yell, "Over here."

Nick lifted his head. Two uniformed cops crowded the doorway while an EMT lurked behind them.

Lacey took Nick's hand and held it against the cloth on his head. Had she used her shirt as a bandage? Maybe he could convince her to use her bra as a tourniquet.

"You have to go after him." Grabbing her sweater from the floor, she jumped up and faced the older officer. "The man who attacked us took off down the stairwell."

The EMTs surged through the door and plucked Lacey's shirt from Nick's head. He tried to sit up, but they wouldn't allow it. Damned cocky EMTs. He preferred the topless nurse.

"Who are we looking for?" The cop pulled a notepad from his pocket and flipped it open.

"A tall man." Lacey stuffed her arms into her sweater and buttoned it up the front before holding her hand well above her own head. "Stocky build, dressed in black with a black ski mask over his face and gloves. I doubt if he left any fingerprints in here."

"A ski mask?" The cop tapped a pencil against his notebook. "Shackleford, check it out."

When Shackleford took off down the hallway, the other officer asked, "What happened? What'd he want?"

"I came up here from Antonio's Deli to deliver a sandwich, and this guy and another guy were rolling around the floor fighting." The pimply kid with an Antonio's Deli cap askew on his head waved his arms around. "Then he pushed past me and stepped on the sandwich."

"Officer—" she leaned forward to peer at the cop's badge "—Bates, the man killed my boss, Dr. Buonfoglio. He's in the back."

Jesus. Nick's gut constricted. He didn't even know Dr. Buonfoglio was in the office. The fight with the masked man just took on a more sinister aspect…and a more deadly one.

At Lacey's words, the paramedics working on Nick abandoned him and rushed to the back while Officer Bates radioed for homicide detectives. Nick took the opportunity to stagger to his feet and immediately dropped to the chair. He'd lost more blood than he'd thought.

"Okay, let's take this from the top." The cop's gaze darted between Nick and Lacey, settling on Lacey. "Who are you, and what's your name?"

"My name is Lacey Kirk, and I'm Dr. Buonfoglio's office manager." She smoothed her auburn hair back from her face, leaving a smudge of blood on her cheek. His or Dr. Buonfoglio's?

As she told Officer Bates about the events leading up to the fight, her voice remained steady and calm, but her hands trembled until she clasped them in front of her.

Nick eased himself out of the chair. "You need to sit down, Lacey. Is there any water in here?"

"Don't touch anything in the office, Doc. Homicide's on their way and they'll want a pristine murder site."

Lacey's pale face blanched further, and she swayed forward.

Nick took her arm and led her to the chair next to the one he just left. "Can I run back to my office to get her some water and a sedative?"

The officer held up his hand. "What's your involvement? Were you in the office, too?"

"No. My office is down the hall. I was on my way back to my office after dropping off some files in the lobby. I heard Lacey screaming and ran in here."

After Nick answered a few more questions, he jogged down the hallway to his office.

When he returned with a cup of water and a couple of sample packets of Xanax, the cop who took off after the masked intruder had returned, and the two paramedics huddled in the corner of the room ready to pounce on him.

"Is Dr. Buonfoglio dead?" He handed Lacey the paper cup and the packets. Her fingers brushed his as she accepted the water, and his nerve endings tingled in response. His adrenaline must still be pumping after that fight.

One of the paramedics nodded. "Yeah, blow to the head. He lost a lot of blood, and so did you. We need to finish with your vitals."

"I'm all right." He traced a fingertip along the angry red mark across the soft creamy skin of Lacey's neck. "You should have a look at her. The guy had his arm locked around her throat when I came in."

"I'll check her out, and my partner can have a look at you." The paramedic shrugged. "The guy in the back doesn't need us. He's ready for the coroner."

"Do you have to be so cold? That's my boss back there." Lacey sniffled and pressed her hands to her cheeks.

"What are they teaching you guys in school about appropriate bedside manner these days?" Nick ran a hand down Lacey's arm and cupped her elbow. After months of watching her whiz back and forth along the hallway and spotting her occasionally at the hospital, now that he was this close to her he had a strong urge to touch her.

She glanced up at him through wet lashes and flashed him a look of gratitude. He squeezed her elbow and allowed the paramedic to check his blood pressure.

Soon after, the office buzzed with enough cops, detectives and crime-scene personnel to populate six of those CSI shows, and more filled the hallway.

Lacey, sitting on the chair beside him, leaned her head back and closed her eyes. Her lashes lay like velvet crescents on her cheeks, and her brown hair with the reddish tint created a silky fan on the cushion. In fact, everything about her had the appearance of softness, until she opened her mouth. Were her sharp comments and sharper looks at the hospital due to his reputation as a player?

That reputation attracted a certain type of woman. The type of woman he always cultivated. The type of woman that represented safety.

Lacey's eyes flew open. "How's your head? I think you lost consciousness. You might have a concussion. You should get it checked out."

"Okay Dr. Lacey."

"Are you one of those doctors who can't take medical advice from others, especially nurses?" She crossed her arms and scowled.

"I have the utmost respect for nurses." He put his hands up to ward off the quills. Did he have to watch everything he said around her? "Couldn't live without them."

She snorted. "Yeah, that's what I heard."

Ouch. One of those quills hit pay dirt. "Don't believe everything you hear."

Why defend himself? He should be pushing this one

away with both hands. Those bright green eyes of hers didn't miss a thing.

Detective Harley Chu, the lead detective on the scene, sat on the edge of the table across from their chairs. "Did the man have a gun?"

"If he did, I didn't see it." Nick shot a look at Lacey. "I thought Dr. Buonfoglio died from blunt trauma to the head."

"He did, but on the other side of his head, there's a mark that looks like the butt of a gun, and Dr. Buonfoglio had his gun in his hand when he went down."

So the good doctor had a gun. That didn't surprise Nick. "I didn't hear any gunfire. Did Dr. Buonfoglio shoot his weapon?"

"No, he never released the safety. Looks like the intruder hit the doctor with the butt of a gun, stunning him. Then he grabbed the bookend and went in for the kill. He probably didn't use his gun on you or Ms. Kirk because of the noise."

Lacey sat up straight and shook her head. "He could've shot us."

Nick studied his nails. "So what was he after?"

"Appears to be a case of theft. He smashed the drug cabinet in the supply room, and it looks like there are drugs missing." Detective Chu tapped his chin with his pencil. He looked over at Lacey. "Do you have an inventory of drugs?"

Nick exhaled. A simple case of theft. God, he was happy to hear those words. Much better than the alternative.

"I do keep a drug inventory on my computer, but the man didn't have a bag or anything, did he, Nick?"

At least the upheaval of the afternoon had prompted her to call him Nick instead of…Dr. Perfect. He drew in a quick breath. She'd called him Dr. Perfect when she was tending to his wound. Smart-ass.

He cleared his throat. "I didn't notice anything, but you know how small the sample packs can be. He could've shoved several of them in his pockets, and he was wearing a big jacket, big enough to conceal anything."

"If he came here to steal, why'd he kill Dr. B?" She drew her bottom lip between her teeth, a furrow creasing her brow.

"He probably thought the office was empty. Maybe he watched you leave and tried the door, and then Dr. Buonfoglio pulled a gun on him." Detective Chu shook his head. "He could've been high already."

"Just seems like a calculated theft with the ski mask and the gloves. And if he was high, it was PCP, because the guy had incredible strength." She niggled her lower lip, obviously not satisfied with the detective's first stab at a motive.

Nick wanted to believe Detective Chu. He had to believe him. It couldn't be what he'd feared for the past three years.

When the coroner arrived, Detective Chu told Lacey she could leave. "You can come back in tomorrow, Ms. Kirk, and check your inventory against what's left in the drug cabinet. You'll probably want to contact Dr. Buonfoglio's patients as well. He's a plastic surgeon, right?"

"Oh, my God." She smacked her forehead. "Dr. B has a surgery tomorrow."

"You can refer the patient to me. In fact, you can refer all of his patients to me for now." Nick stood up and massaged his left shoulder. He'd convinced the paramedics he didn't need to go to the hospital, but he could use some painkillers and a good night's sleep.

"I didn't realize you needed the work." Lacey skewered him with a sideways glance.

He must've done her wrong in a past life or something. Should he even bother to remedy her low opinion of him? He shrugged. "Just trying to help out."

"Thanks." She tucked an errant strand of hair behind her ear. "But this particular patient tomorrow is top secret."

"Huh?" Her words punched him in the gut. Dr. Buonfoglio had top-secret patients? Seems the good doctor still played with fire...probably why he had a gun.

"You know, celebrities, politicians. You don't have the corner on that market yet, Dr. Per...Marino."

He raised his eyebrows, but her words untied the knot in his belly. That explained the "secret patients." All cosmetic surgeons had them. "It's Marino, not Per-Marino."

A pink tide ebbed into her cheeks as she covered her mouth with her hand. "I know that."

Nailed her.

She turned to the detective. "Detective Chu, should I notify Dr. B's surgical nurses? His bookkeeper works off-site. I should notify her, too."

"You need to give us those names and addresses, and we'll notify them. We have to interview them, anyway. Do you want an officer to accompany you to your car?"

"I'll walk her down." Nick stepped forward. "Get those names for Detective Chu while I pick up a few things from my office."

Her eyes widened, but she kept her mouth shut for a change. Seems his take-charge attitude could overwhelm even Lacey Kirk, Nurse Know-It-All. He'd developed that attitude years ago, even before he became a doctor. It was an essential component in keeping things from spinning out of control.

By the time he got back, Lacey was waiting for him, clutching her blood-stained shirt in her hand.

"I'll replace that for you."

"This?" She waved it in front of her. "Don't worry about it. It's just a Target special."

He draped his suit jacket over his arm and gestured her ahead of him into the hallway.

Her gaze dropped to the Armani jacket, and then meandered up his silk tie and tailored shirt, now ripped and smudged with blood.

"I suppose you didn't realize Target even had a clothing line, did you?"

Definite porcupine. He grabbed her arm and lied. "Yes, I did know that. Is the SFPD going to lock up Dr. Buonfoglio's office?"

"Yeah." She shook him off. "They're putting one of those lock boxes on the door, like Realtors use. A cop's going to be waiting for me tomorrow to unlock it when I come in to check things out and notify Dr. B's patients."

When they got into the elevator, Lacey leaned her forehead against the wall, her shoulders slumping. "I can't believe this happened."

"Dr. Buonfoglio was a good man and a good doctor. He'll be missed." He rubbed her back, and although she stiffened beneath his touch, she didn't pull away.

The elevator landed on the second floor of the parking garage, and the doors rumbled open. Empty stalls yawned before them, and Lacey's heels resounded through the cavernous lot.

Her small red Jetta stood alone in one row. Lacey took out her keys, and the Jetta's lights flashed once.

"What's this? Did I get a ticket for being in the parking structure too long?" She strode ahead of him and plucked a piece of paper from beneath her windshield wipers.

Holding the scrap of paper in her hands, she glanced back at Nick, her mouth dropping open. "D-do you think *he* left this?"

His stride devoured the space between them, and with a muscle ticking in his jaw, he snatched the paper from her hand.

Two circles with dots in the middle, resembling a pair of eyes, stared back at him. The blood pounded in his head, his wound beneath the paramedics' expert bandage throbbing with each beat. He crushed the piece of paper in his fist.

They'd come back.
They meant business.
And they wanted his brother.

Chapter Two

"Nick?" She ran her fingers over his white knuckles. "Are you all right? Do you need to sit down?"

He jerked his head up, his dark eyes focusing on her face, as if he'd been in a place far away.

"I'm okay. Just felt a little dizzy." He unwrapped the crumpled piece of paper and smoothed it out on the hood of her car.

"Do you think it's a message from the man who murdered Dr. B? I know this paper wasn't on my car when I came down here before." Her gaze slid to the circles, and a chill snaked up her spine.

"It could be."

His color had returned to its normal olive complexion, but his tight jaw signaled some distress. The stubborn oaf should've let the paramedics take him to the hospital. Doctors always thought they knew better than every other medical professional...especially Dr. Perfect.

To keep from smoothing her hands across his worried brow, she slid the piece of paper from beneath his hand and lifted it between two fingers. "Looks like eyes. Do you think that means he's watching me?"

She looked over her shoulder, peering into the dimly lit recesses of the parking garage. Her heart fluttered, and she tried to beat back the fear. She'd never lived her life in fear, even when her dad left the family, and she didn't intend to start now.

"How'd he pick out my car, anyway?" She rolled her shoulders. "Maybe this is just a coincidence, a joke."

"It's not hard to figure out." Nick pointed to the office-suite numbers painted on her parking space and the two empty ones beside her car. "Yours is the only car here, and even if the guy doesn't know that the doctors park on the first level, I don't know many doctors who drive Jettas."

She rolled her eyes. "You are such a snob. Even in times of crisis, you don't forget the medical hierarchy."

He slammed his fist on the roof of her car. "Can you forget your own insecurities for two seconds while we work this through?"

She swallowed. The suave Dr. Perfect just morphed into this Nick Marino character with flashing dark eyes and a hard jaw. Like steel encased in velvet. It suddenly became clear why nobody messed with him at the hospital. Apparently, he possessed weapons other than charm in his arsenal of persuasion.

"Sure, I'm sorry."

"I'm sorry, too." He rubbed his eyes and dragged his long fingers through thick, dark hair. "You've been through a lot today, and I'm standing here yelling at you."

He opened her car door for her and nudged her back. "Go home and get some rest. Do you still have the Xanax I gave you? Take one."

"What about this?" She waved the paper in his face. "Shouldn't we tell Detective Chu about this?"

"I'll go back up to the office and give it to him. The guy may have done it to scare you. Detective Chu's probably right. He's a drug addict hopped up on something."

"I hope so." She hugged herself, pulling her sweater tight. "I'm no threat to him. I can't identify him, but if he left any evidence on the note that can be traced, it's important that Chu see it. I want this guy caught. I want him to pay for what he did to Dr. B, and I'll help any way I can."

Nick put the note in the pocket of his slacks. "I doubt this piece of paper will help the detectives, but it's worth a try. Get some sleep. I'll check in on you tomorrow at the office, and remember, send Dr. B's patients to me. If I can't help them, I'll refer them out."

She slid onto the seat of the car and locked the doors. As she cruised out of the parking structure, she saw Nick in her rearview mirror, following her on foot. She drove slowly, and as she pulled up to the parking arm and slid her card key into the slot, Nick caught up with her bumper and slapped the trunk.

She wheeled onto the rain-slicked street. Nick lifted his hand, and she waved back.

Nick showed some real guts and heart today. Maybe Dr. Perfect had more depth than she ever imagined…and he was even better-looking up close and personal.

THE FOLLOWING MORNING, Lacey dragged her feet down the hallway toward the office with the yellow police tape criss-crossed over the doorway. A uniformed officer lounged nearby, talking to one of Nick's office nurses, Petra. Lacey squared her shoulders. After yesterday's terror and a sleep-less night, she didn't need one of Petra's inquisitions. She wanted to get away from this office and return to the safety of her own home.

"Oh, my God, Lacey, you must've been terrified. Are you okay?" Petra hugged her, patting her back.

"My throat's a little sore, but other than that, I'm fine. Dr. B didn't fare so well." Tears stung her nose and she rubbed it with a tissue.

"I know. I feel just awful…."

Petra trailed off. Dr. B was not known for his sparkling personality or great wit. He kept to himself, a morose, solitary man. The police notified his daughter in New Jersey, and Lacey had spoken with her on the phone this morning. She planned to fly his body back to Jersey for the funeral and burial.

The young officer cleared his throat. "Are you Lacey Kirk?"

"Yeah, do you need to see some ID or something?" She fumbled in her purse and drew out her wallet with her driver's license.

He looked it over and unlocked the box attached to the office door.

"Can you believe that Nick came into the office today?" Petra shook her head. "He told us all about how he came to your rescue and chased off the bad guy, and he came in to work today even with that bandage on the side of his head."

"He didn't exactly chase off the bad guy." Leave it to Dr. Perfect to put the perfect spin on the story. She blew out a breath. But he probably saved her life, and she never even thanked him for it. "He did come to my rescue, though."

Petra sighed. "Must be nice."

"To be choked by a murderer?"

"Oh, no, of course not." Petra blinked and flapped her hands.

Lacey ducked under the police tape. She licked her lips as she surveyed the upended furniture and bloodstains in the reception area. Nick's blood.

"Can I straighten this out now?"

The cop answered, "Sure. They're done collecting evidence."

"Are you going to wait in the hallway? You're welcome to hang out here."

"I'm okay." He grinned at Petra.

She snapped the door shut. Great, the murderer could be lurking in here, and her only protection was flirting with a nurse in the hallway.

Her gaze darted to the door leading to the back rooms. When did Dr. B hear the intruder? If he had a gun, why didn't he just shoot him when the guy came into his office? Maybe the murderer came in with his gun pulled first. Thank God he didn't shoot her...or Nick.

Holding her breath, she crept through the door. The fax machine started churning, and she jumped. She watched a piece of paper slide into the fax tray. She froze. What if the killer faxed her a set of eyes?

She tiptoed to the fax machine and lifted the paper. An ad for a medical supply company. She shook her head and crumpled the single sheet. *Get a grip.*

Avoiding Dr. B's office, she entered the supply room. Shards of glass from the cabinets littered the floor, and a caustic aroma rose from the sink, cluttered with broken bottles of medicine. Time to make that list of missing drugs for Detective Chu.

She returned to the reception area and pulled out the chair at her desk, perching on its edge. She'd never feel comfortable in this office again, which didn't pose much of a problem since she'd probably never come back.

Dr. B worked alone, no partners. His two surgical nurses had been with him for years, as had his bookkeeper. Lacey had spoken to both of his nurses, Debbie Chase and Jill Zombrotto, last night. Detective Chu had already notified them, so the initial shock had worn off—at least for Debbie, the stoic one. Jill had always been more emotional, and she was still crying when Lacey spoke to her.

Their dedication to Dr. B never wavered, and Lacey wasn't quite sure what they got in return. They probably could've earned more money at a busier practice, and they didn't stick around for Dr. B's jovial personality.

Dr. B valued privacy, especially after his wife, Rose, died.

Lacey's mom and Rose shared the same oncologist and became friendly in the waiting room. When Mom found out Rose's husband needed a receptionist, she suggested Lacey. Rose had asked them to dinner a few times, so Lacey could meet Dr. B. She needed the job while she finished her last year of the hospice program, which she began after Mom's cancer came back.

Mom passed away first, and Rose followed six months later. Dr. B didn't need Lacey for emotional support after his wife died, but he still needed her office and nursing skills. He always kept to himself and frustrated her efforts at caretaking...even at the very end. She couldn't do a thing to save him.

She powered on her computer and opened the database containing all of Dr. B's patients, except the top-secret ones. Jill and Debbie could handle those.

After printing out an inventory of drugs in the office, she made several calls to give his patients the bad news. Many of them had already heard about the murder on TV or read about it in the newspaper. When they asked for a referral, she gave them Dr. Nick Marino's name. He'd offered, hadn't he?

She took care of other details to close down the office. His daughter could handle the logistics of his practice...and her sister. Dr. B's other daughter, Abby, had Down syndrome and resided in a group home in Santa Cruz. She hoped the police would leave it to her sister to tell Abby the news.

She reached for her keys in the purse she'd hung on the back of her chair. Damn, she never did lock her desk last night. If she hadn't forgotten, she never would've come back up here. The guy never would've attacked her. Nick never would've saved her.

She jerked open the middle desk drawer and frowned. She'd left the appointment book right on top last night. Not that she needed it. The book simply duplicated the database, because Dr. B preferred reviewing his appointments on paper rather than logging on to his computer. And Dr. B wouldn't be reviewing appointments anymore.

"I'm going to grab some lunch downstairs. Are you okay?" The uniformed officer poked his head in the door. "Do you want me to get something for you?"

The thought of eating anything in this office turned her stomach. She declined his offer and searched the next drawer for the appointment book. Maybe Dr. B took it to his office last night.

She took a deep breath and pushed out of her chair. It felt as if her ankles had chains attached to them as she dragged her feet to Dr. B's office.

The red stain on the carpet in front of his desk still looked damp. She edged around the other side, nudging his chair out of the way with her knee. The filing cabinet next to his desk, the one he kept locked, had been pried open. It contained the blue file folders for the doctor's special patients, the ones who didn't want to be identified. She ran her fingers along the tabs, but couldn't tell if the intruder took anything from the cabinet.

She turned toward his desk and opened each drawer, searching through the contents. Dr. B kept a messy desk, but the disorder in the drawers topped anything she'd seen before.

The killer had searched the filing cabinet and the desk. If he wanted drugs, why look here? Maybe he wanted money or a prescription pad, too.

"Looking for something?"

She jumped, jerking the drawer out, its contents spilling on the floor. Nick's large frame filled the doorway as he propped a shoulder against the doorjamb. His white coat billowed open to reveal another expensive shirt and silk tie. The man could grace the cover of *GQ*.

"You scared me." She crouched to gather the junk from the drawer off the floor. "How'd you get in here?"

"The officer in the hallway let me in. Seems he and my nurse, Petra, have formed a close bond."

She thumbed through the papers and notebooks before dropping them back in the drawer and picking up another stack. No appointment book.

"Petra works fast."

"So do you."

She sliced her finger on a paper edge. "What?"

"You're back in here so soon after the murder to take care of everything. Where are Dr. Buonfoglio's surgical nurses?"

"They were with him a long time." She shoved the drawer back into the desk and stood up, sucking on her finger. "I spoke with them last night, and they're shocked. They need a few days to recover before coming in here." Especially Jill.

"Did you hurt your finger?" He stepped forward and held out his hand.

"It's just a paper cut, Doc."

"Let me see it, anyway." He cupped his outstretched hand and gestured her forward.

Might as well humor the guy. He obviously had no problem taking charge of a situation, and recalling the way he flew through the door of the office last night to attack the intruder, she didn't have a problem with it, either.

She held out her hand, and he wrapped his long fingers around her wrist and peered at the slice on her finger that sported a tiny drop of blood. He had beautiful hands—surgeon's hands—strong, capable, deft. She stopped. The surgeon's hands last night delivered punishing blows, showing strength of another kind...brute strength.

"Dab some antiseptic on this and get a Band-Aid. The man last night didn't steal all your Band-Aids, did he?"

She snatched her hand back. "I'm sure we have some in the examination room."

"So what did he steal?"

She skirted past him and rounded the corner into the examination room. He followed.

"I'm sure he stole some drugs. I still have to compare my inventory against the mess he left behind and give a list to Detective Chu." And the appointment book? She hadn't found it among Dr. B's clutter, either.

She grabbed a Band-Aid and spun around, meeting Nick's dark eyes.

"Something else?" His brows rose.

"Last night you said the man was wearing a jacket big enough to conceal anything. Big enough to hide an eight-by-eleven notebook?"

"What kind of notebook?" Nick shoved his hands in the pockets of his lab coat and leaned against the wall, as if to strike a casual pose. The gestures failed. His eyes narrowed and his nostrils flared, indicating anything but casual.

What did she expect? He was minding his own business last night, heard her scream and jumped into a life-and-death struggle.

"An appointment book." She squared her hands in front of her. "I can't find my appointment book."

His shoulders relaxed. "You still keep an appointment book? Don't you have a database on your computer?"

"I keep both. Dr. B liked to see his appointments on paper, all collected in one book."

"Just names and dates, that kind of thing?" He flicked a piece of lint off his spotless sleeve.

Why was Dr. Nick Marino suddenly developing an interest in Dr. Buonfoglio's method of keeping appointments? Well, even if he cultivated pretense, she didn't.

"Yeah, names and phone numbers penciled in on a calendar. Why are you so interested?"

His eyes widened. "Why wouldn't I be? A doctor on my floor, another cosmetic surgeon, is murdered and I'm supposed to take it in stride? Shrug it off?"

She bit her lip. He had a point. She was supposed to be the caring hospice nurse and he the coldhearted, money-grubbing cosmetic surgeon.

"I'm sorry, Nick. You have every right to be concerned, and I never even thanked you for saving my life."

He shrugged. "As a cosmetic surgeon, I don't get to save a life every day. Do you need help with the inventory?"

"What about your patients? Don't you need to get back to work?"

"I canceled all my appointments for the rest of the day." He pointed to the bandage on his head. "I'm afraid this didn't inspire much confidence in my patients this morning."

She accepted his help, and after she grabbed the inventory list off her desk, they snapped on matching rubber gloves to sort through the mess in the supply room. She checked off each item and quantity on her list as Nick pieced together broken bottles and smashed containers.

When Nick swept up the last of the glass from the floor, Lacey sat back on her heels and frowned. "I don't get it."

"What?" He dumped the contents of the dustpan into the trash bin they'd ordered from Facilities.

"There's really not that much missing from this list." She tapped the pen on the paper. "It just looked like he stole a lot because he trashed the place."

"Maybe he grabbed the easy-to-steal sample packets. Do you keep an inventory of those? I don't. Maybe you interrupted him before he could get down to business."

"Why did he smash everything if he was looking for drugs to steal? Unless…" She stood up and lodged a shoulder against the doorjamb.

"Unless what?" Nick looked up sharply.

"Unless he just wanted it to look like he was after the drugs."

He banged the lid on the trash can and leaned over it, not turning around to look at her. "What was he after, Nancy Drew?"

Why did he sound so angry with her? The fumes must've gone to his head. "I don't know, but he thought he might find it in Dr. B's desk."

"Was anything missing other than the appointment book?" He turned slowly, still gripping the trash can behind him.

"Not that I could tell. Are you okay? Maybe it wasn't such a great idea for you to be crouching over for an hour cleaning up with that head injury."

He plowed a hand through his hair, careful to avoid his bandage. "I'm starving. How about you? Do you want to join me for lunch?"

"Sure, but let me pay since you helped me out here…and for last night. I can't face Antonio's. Can we walk down the street a little to the Chinese place?"

"It's a deal." He peeled off the gloves and dropped them into the trash.

When Nick opened the office door for her, the cop on duty stepped to the side, still talking to Petra. Petra's gaze darted between the two of them, a red tide washing across her face.

"I didn't know you were in there, Dr. Marino. Since we don't have any patients today, I figured I'd return some calls and phone in a few prescriptions. I'm just taking a break."

"No problem." He shrugged out of his lab coat. "Can you hang this up for me when you get back to the office? Lacey and I are grabbing some lunch."

Hugging the coat to her chest, Petra raised her brows over a pair of inquisitive blue eyes that Lacey could feel burning into the back of her head until she turned the corner to the elevator. Nick generated a lot of interest and speculation among the women at the office and the hospital.

Well, let them speculate. The least she could do was to buy him lunch. He came to her aid last night and helped out again today. Who would've suspected Dr. Marino of having a chivalrous streak?

They trudged uphill on the damp sidewalk, and a slice of blue San Francisco Bay rewarded their efforts when they got to the top. Last night's rain rinsed the sky clean, leaving a few puffy white clouds tumbling in the breeze.

The afternoon lunch rush had long since cleared out, and only a few tables of tourists remained in the restaurant when they got there.

Keeping that chivalry thing going, Nick pulled out her chair. It had been a while since a man pulled out her chair on a date. Who was she kidding? It had been a while since she'd been on a date. Not that she considered this a date.

"Do you like it spicy?"

He quirked a brow, looking ten kinds of suave, and warmth flooded her cheeks. Good thing this wasn't a date.

"The food…I mean, do you like spicy food?"

"Yeah, I do." He shook open the plastic menu. "I've never been here before. What do you recommend?"

She rattled off a few dishes, careful to stick to the lunch menu. Either he took the hint about her budget, or his mama raised him right, because he ordered one of the cheapest lunch specials.

She poured tea for both of them. "Did you grow up in the Bay Area or are you a transplant like so many others?"

"I'm afraid I'm a transplant but an early one. I moved here when I was eleven. How about you?"

"California native. My parents moved here from Chicago."

"Does your family still live here?"

"No. My mom died almost a year ago, and my brother, Ryan, is a marine stationed with a peacekeeping force in Kosovo."

He put down his teacup, keeping his hands wrapped around it. "I'm sorry about your mom. What about your dad?"

She'd never met a man who asked so many questions, especially a doctor. Usually they blabbed on about themselves and their marvelous achievements.

"Do you really want to hear my sad story?"

"Only if you want to tell it. I respect people's privacy. That's part of my job."

She looked into his dark eyes, eyes that invited confidences but gave nothing back. Eyes that encouraged patients to open up about their fears and insecurities about their looks and their deepest desires for love, acceptance and eternal youth.

"My dad was having an affair, and when my mom got sick he just up and left us for the other woman. Then he moved to Florida with the other woman and started a whole new family with her." She paused as the waiter set down their dishes. "Mom was a nurse and Dad's a doctor."

"Oh. Do you want to share entrées?" When she nodded, he served her first and then himself. "When did your father leave? You said your mom died a year ago."

"My dad left when my brother and I were teenagers. Guess he figured he'd owe less child support. Mom was diagnosed with cancer then, went into remission and had a relapse two years ago."

"Ah, that explains the specialty in palliative care."

"Am I that transparent? Why did you become a doctor?"

"The usual reasons." He lifted a broad shoulder. "I know the nurse who runs your program, May Pritchard. How do you like it?"

And just like that, he had her describing the program and explaining how she was a medical assistant and decided to return to school. By the time she paid the fifteen-dollar bill plus tax and tip, she realized she didn't know a damn thing about Dr. Nick Marino other than the paltry facts that he moved to California when he was eleven and became a doctor for "the usual reasons," whatever that meant—probably money, judging by his specialty and lifestyle.

When they stepped off the elevator on their floor, Lacey extended her hand. "I'm going the other way to hit the ladies' room. Thanks for all your help, Nick. I'll probably be back in here a few more times, and then I'll leave Dr. B's office for his daughter to settle. Maybe I'll see you around the hospital."

"I hope so, Lacey." He squeezed her hand and then disappeared around the corner.

She fished the key to the ladies' room out of her purse and slid it into the lock. "I hope so" didn't sound very promising, but then what did she expect? He probably listened to her go on about the nursing program because he felt sorry for her, or worse, he had an interest in May Pritchard, an attractive redhead.

As she washed her hands, the door swung open and Petra stepped into the restroom.

"How was your lunch?"

"It was fine. I wanted to repay Nick for coming to the rescue last night and helping me out today."

"Just be careful." Petra's eyes met hers in the mirror.

"Be careful? I don't have anything to worry about. I didn't see the intruder's face. I can't identify him, and I doubt he could identify me."

Petra rolled her eyes. "Not about that. I mean watch yourself with Nick. He's a player. Total love-'em-and-leave-'em kind of guy. He'll date a woman two, maybe three times, and that's it. Nobody gets close to Dr. Nick Marino."

"I'm safe." She swiped her lipstick across her lips with an unsteady hand. "I'm not interested in getting close."

Lacey shoved out of the ladies' room. The last thing she needed was another arrogant doctor in her life. She chose nursing because of Mom, but vowed not to make the same mistake as her mother by dating doctors. She worked with them—that's it.

She turned the corner to find a cluster of people at the office doorway. Detective Chu and Nick looked up at the same time wearing matching frowns, only Nick looked more serious than the detective.

Lacey's heart skittered in her chest, and she took a deep breath. Detective Chu probably just wanted the list of missing narcotics, but why had he shown up in person to get it?

"Did you come by for the inventory, Detective?" Lacey crossed her arms, hugging her purse to her chest.

"I'll take it, but I think the killer may have been after more than drugs, Lacey."

Her gaze darted to Nick, who stood stiffly beside her, his own arms crossed over his chest.

"H-how do you know?"

Detective Chu rubbed his jaw and expelled a breath. "Someone murdered Debbie Chase this morning."

Chapter Three

"M-murdered?" Lacey took a step back and held up her hands, as if to ward off Detective Chu's words…and their meaning.

Nick dug his fingers into his arms to keep from reaching out and holding her. Both she and the detective would find his response unwarranted and over the top, but Lacey didn't know the menace that threatened her, and neither did Detective Chu. He had to keep her in the dark for her own safety.

Could he protect her and his brother, too?

"Oh, my God." She covered her face with her hands. "How did Debbie die?"

"She was strangled." Detective Chu lifted the police tape and ushered Lacey through, her fingers tracing the bruise on her throat. "Let's go in here to discuss this."

Nick followed them. He had to find out as much information as he could. Lacey's life depended on it, and so did his brother's.

"What does he want? It can't be the drugs." Lacey paced the carpet, twisting her hands in front of her.

"I'm not sure, but he's definitely looking for something, and he's desperate to find it. He tore apart Debbie's house."

"I guess he didn't find it in the appointment book."

Detective Chu looked up from his notes. "Appointment book?"

Nick sucked in a breath. How far would this investigation go? How far could he let it go? He didn't want any more people to suffer, but he didn't want the cops to get any more leads. He had to do this on his own. If only Dr. Buonfoglio's secrets had died with him, but someone out there believed at least one of his surgical nurses shared those secrets. And what about Lacey?

He watched her as she told Chu everything she'd discovered today—the missing appointment book, Dr. B's ransacked desk and the full inventory of drugs. She didn't know anything, and Nick intended to keep it that way.

"So I thought it was odd. If the guy wanted drugs, why did he smash everything? What's he looking for?" She spread her arms wide.

"Did the doctor have any enemies, any lawsuits going on? Any botched surgeries?" Chu tapped his notebook.

Snapping his fingers, Nick said, "Sometimes a patient believes something went wrong with the surgery, but doesn't have a case for a lawsuit. Cosmetic surgery is subjective in many instances. It could be a patient, dissatisfied with his surgery, trying to get something on him."

He wanted to steer Chu in as many wrong directions as possible. If he could just buy some time, he might be able to salvage the situation and protect everyone involved. Then he'd give the SFPD and the FBI just enough information to bring the killer—and those who hired him—to justice.

"It must be someone who's familiar with the office. How would he know about Debbie and where she lived?" Lacey stopped wearing a hole in the carpet and clutched her stomach. "He's watching me, too."

"Someone's watching you?" Chu asked.

"The eyes." She waved her arms. "The eyes on my car last night." She turned to Nick. "You did bring that piece of paper back up to Detective Chu after I left last night, didn't you?"

Nick nodded. Even though he didn't want to show those eyes to Chu, he'd given him the note.

"I'm going to be sick." Lacey's creamy complexion turned a waxy white as she clutched her midsection.

"Sit down." Nick took one flailing arm and led Lacey to a chair. "I'll get you some water."

As Nick filled a disposable cup from the water dispenser, Detective Chu said, "We don't know that, Lacey. That paper with the eyes could've come from anyone. We don't even know if those were supposed to be eyes."

She thanked Nick for the water and took a sip, the whiteness around her lips receding.

"They looked like eyes to me, Detective." She shook her head, her silky dark hair falling over one shoulder. "He plans to watch me just as he watched Debbie, like he's probably watching Jill. Am I next?"

"That depends on what you know, or what he thinks you know, and we've already contacted Jill Zombrotto to tell her to be careful."

"This is all just speculation." Nick jumped up between Detective Chu and Lacey. He had to stop this line of questioning. "It could just be some nut job, a disgruntled patient or the relative of one. Maybe Dr. Buonfoglio gave some woman a younger face and a breast augmentation and she left her husband for the cabana boy. Now her husband's taking it out on the doctor and searched the office to make it look like a burglary."

Detective Chu's eyebrows shot up and Lacey's jaw dropped as she stared at him. Okay, maybe he should back off, or he'd have Detective Chu investigating him. And he couldn't have that. Ever.

"I think you're stretching it, Nick." Lacey's brow creased. "What did Jill have to say? Did she seem to think Dr. B had something to hide?" Lacey's knee bounced up and down, the water sloshing over the side of the paper cup and onto her jeans.

Chu's lips twisted. "Actually, she had the same response as Dr. Marino—disgruntled patient."

Nick massaged the back of his neck. Either that nurse had an active imagination or she had as much to hide as he did.

Detective Chu finished questioning Lacey, but she had nothing to add to the speculation.

Nick's pulse quickened when Chu asked her about the special patients who slipped in and out of the office incognito.

"I don't know much about them…." She stopped and smacked her forehead with the heel of her hand. "I forgot. The guy broke into Dr. B's locked filing cabinet, the one that contained the files for those special patients."

The blood pounded in Nick's ears as his heart hammered. He turned his back on Lacey and Chu and got some water, schooling the tension out of his tight face.

Chu asked, "Was anything missing?"

"Not that I could tell, but Deb…I mean Jill will have a better idea."

Closing his eyes, Nick gulped the water and then took in a deep breath. Even though Dr. Buonfoglio lived life on the edge, there was no way he'd keep sensitive files in a locked filing cabinet in his office. Why had he kept those records at all?

"Can you do another search of Dr. Buonfoglio's files to see if anything's missing? We'll have Ms. Zombrotto come into the office tomorrow and check out that filing cabinet. Maybe between the two of you, we can find out what this guy's after."

"C-can you offer any protection, Detective Chu?"

Lacey's wide green eyes got wider, and her hands gripped the arms of the chair as if she was ready for takeoff. Nick's gut twisted. Those bastards ruined lives, but he'd be damned if he'd let them touch anyone close to him again.

"I'm afraid we don't have the manpower for that." He stuffed his notebook back in his pocket. "Just be aware of your surroundings. Get the security guard to escort you down to your car. Officer Bennett will be stationed outside the office until you and Ms. Zombrotto finish your search of the files."

Nick jumped to his feet. As if an unarmed security guard could protect her. He'd have to take his own measures. "If you're ready to leave now, Lacey, I'll walk you down."

Her gaze darted around the room, and she pressed her fingers to her temples. "I think I will leave now. I'll come back in tomorrow when Jill's here, and we can look through Dr. B's stuff together."

After she locked her desk and gave Chu the inventory, they stepped into the hallway and Officer Bennett secured the door behind them.

"Wait here while I check in with my office." Nick held up his hand, and then jogged to his office.

Zoe, his receptionist, looked up as he burst through the door. "Dr. Marino, are you coming back in? I canceled all your appointments."

"No, I'm not in to see patients, but I'll be back up to do some work and you can put calls through." He strode to his office and slammed the door behind him. He plucked his jacket from the hook on the back of the door and shrugged into it. Then he crouched behind his desk, unlocking it, and pulled open the bottom drawer. He didn't even check to see if the gun was loaded before slipping it into the pocket of his jacket. He always kept a loaded gun with him. Old habits died hard.

"I'll be right back." He waved to Zoe on his way out the door.

His shallow breathing returned to normal when he saw Lacey talking to the cop in front of Dr. Buonfoglio's office. She obviously had no clue about the types of surgeries her boss occasionally performed, but the surgical nurses knew.

How long before the remaining nurse, Jill Zombrotto, spilled the beans to the cops, or worse, the FBI? She'd be in hot water herself, so maybe she'd decide to take her chances with the other side. Nick couldn't allow her to take any chances.

He might just have to pay a visit to Jill Zombrotto himself.

LACEY STACKED THE LAST of the dinner dishes for one in the dishwasher and dried her hands. She left the pot of chili on the stove to cool off. Lifting her tea bag from her cup, she watched the droplets splash into the amber liquid as she inhaled the cinnamon scent. She eyed the open books on her kitchen table, and then skirted the table on her way to the worn, comfy sofa. She had to do some advance reading for her next class, which started in a week, but had zero concentration.

Just like that, half of the people she worked with were dead. Why? What secrets did Dr. B have that warranted murder?

Lacey curled her legs beneath her on the sofa as she wrapped her hands around her warm cup. Dr. Nick Marino had secrets, too. His dark eyes told a different story from the attractive, easygoing, playboy bachelor about town. They held wariness and pain.

She snorted into her cup. *Like Dr. Perfect needs tea and sympathy from you.* The wariness probably came from being on guard against lusty, gold-digging women. Now that she'd met Nick and broke bread with him, she totally got those women—not the gold-digging part but the lusty part.

When he walked her to the parking garage this afternoon, he dipped his head, his lips hovering so close to hers she almost expected a kiss, and despite her previous disdain for him, she wouldn't have minded one bit.

At lunch he showed more humility than she expected. He

spent the entire lunchtime questioning her, and didn't once mention his burgeoning practice or his graduation from Stanford Medical School at the top of his class.

He took his guardian angel duties seriously, too, sort of like a knight in a white coat instead of on a white horse. Before she ducked into her car, he held her shoulders in a caress and told her to be careful.

She shook her head and slurped her tea. He probably loved this new role, which gave him the chance to play hero to all his adoring female fans.

The ringing phone halted any further thoughts about the mysterious Dr. Marino. She placed her cup on the coffee table, bounded up from the sofa and scooped the phone from the counter. "Hello?"

"Hi, Lacey, it's Jill."

"I'm so happy to hear your voice." Lacey sank back onto the sofa and grabbed a pillow. "I tried to call you earlier when I heard about Debbie."

"I—I was out all day. It just seemed safer." Jill's husky voice almost whispered across the phone line, sending a chill creeping along Lacey's flesh.

"What do you mean, safer? Are you in danger?"

"We're all in danger, Lacey, even you."

"What's this about, Jill?" She dug her fingernails into the pillow. "Who killed Dr. B and Debbie?"

Jill sobbed. "I shouldn't tell you anything, but I can't do this alone. You see, I have the key, not Debbie, not Dr. B. I have it."

"What key?" Jill sounded an inch away from total hysteria. "Tell me what's wrong."

"I could give the key to Lacey. She doesn't know anything. They won't hurt her. She can give the key to the FBI. The FBI won't punish her. She didn't assist in the surgeries."

"Jill." Lacey's voice was as sharp as the pain in the back of her head. She had to bring Jill back from the brink of panic. "Where's the key, Jill? What does it unlock?"

"I keep it with me always, close to my heart. Can I give you the key, Lacey? They won't hurt you. I promise. Or you can go on the run with me. I always wanted a daughter, but they wouldn't let me. I could never have a family. You don't have a family, either. We could be a family, Lacey."

Through her tears, Jill babbled about keys and families and daughters, no longer forming coherent sentences.

"Jill? Hang up the phone and lie down." Lacey spoke with a calmness her trembling hands belied. "I'm on my way over."

With frightening clarity, Jill answered, "They'll kill us. Pack your bag. We're leaving tonight," and then ended the call.

Lacey sat clutching the phone in her lap for a moment, her hands clammy and her mouth dry. The murders of Dr. B and Debbie had hit Jill hard…that's all. The three of them had been together for years. Jill and Debbie didn't have families. They put everything into their work, and naturally Jill felt the loss down to her bones.

That had to be it. Lacey didn't want it to be anything more sinister. After the turbulence of her childhood, she'd plotted and planned her life carefully to follow an even course. Fate couldn't play such a cruel joke on her.

Tossing the pillow to the side, she pushed off the sofa. She replaced the phone in the kitchen and dumped her tea in the sink. Time to act like a nurse.

She grabbed her jacket and dropped the sample pack of Xanax Nick gave her last night into her pocket. Jill needed it a lot more than she did.

The moist air caressed her face as she stepped off the porch of the little house in Sunset her mom bought after she and Dad sold the more luxurious digs in Nob Hill. Dad enjoyed all the flash and image. That's why he left Mom for that young pharmaceutical saleswoman.

The heavy fog rolled off the bay, creating a damp curtain around her as she moved toward the Jetta parked on the street. She'd been to Jill's apartment just once, but she'd looked up the address in her phone book, and its location just up from Fisherman's Wharf would be easy to find.

Thirty-five minutes later, Lacey's car rolled to a stop across the street from Jill's apartment building. The fog, thicker down here, smelled of fish and brine, and she moved into its embrace as she approached the pink stucco building lit by floodlights. She found Jill's name on one of the labels next to the dull gold buttons, which she jabbed with her finger.

Damn, no answer. Had Jill fallen into an exhausted sleep? Maybe she'd been drinking and passed out.

She stepped back and a sliver of light fell across her shoes. Her gaze tracked the light to a crack in the door where someone had wedged it open with a magazine. So much for security measures.

Lacey pushed open the door, slick with moisture, and wiped her hands on her jeans. She wrinkled her nose at the smell of the lobby, musty like old shoes. The elevator doors creaked open. She stepped inside, punching the button to the third floor over and over, as if that could make the old car move faster.

The threadbare carpet in the corridor muffled her steps as she trailed a hand along the wall, peering at apartment numbers etched into brass plates on each door. She reached number 329 at the end of the hallway and tapped on the door. Silence.

If Jill didn't answer, maybe she could get the manager to open the door. She could always claim to be Jill's daughter. After that hysterical phone call, Lacey wanted to check on Jill even if she was sleeping.

She rapped one knuckle on the door while trying the doorknob. The handle turned and Lacey glanced down, catching her bottom lip between her teeth. If Jill was worried about her safety, why'd she leave her door unlocked?

A whisper of fear brushed the back of Lacey's neck as she gripped the door handle. She put her ear to the door, hearing nothing but the resounding beat of her heart.

She nudged the door with her hip and poked her head inside. A Tiffany lamp burned brightly in the corner of the room, throwing triangles of color on the wall.

"Jill?" Lacey stepped into the room, leaving the front door open behind her. She tiptoed forward, sucking in a breath when she saw a desk drawer pulled open and papers scattered across the hardwood floor.

God, not again.

Somewhere in her head, a voice cried, "Run, run, run," but her feet plodded one after the other, moving to another instinct that commanded her to help Jill.

An orange ball of fur rushed past her, skidding to a stop in the bathroom. The cat's plaintive cries echoed throughout the apartment, bringing a rash of goose bumps to Lacey's arms.

She hovered at the entrance to the short hallway, which branched into a bedroom, a bathroom and a closet, its door gaping open. She had a clear view of the bathroom and the orange tabby meowing on the tattered bath rug. The bedroom door stood ajar, an almost palpable menace oozing from its interior. Still her feet carried her forward. The door whined on its hinges as Lacey pushed it open.

Jill's body lay sprawled across the bed, the chintz coverlet clutched in one fist, her eyes bulging from their sockets. Discoloration marked her neck, and her other hand lay across her breast, fingers inches from her throat and the silver chain she always wore.

Lacey brought one of her own fists to her mouth and pressed it against her lips as sour bile rose up her gut. She inched toward the bed and crouched beside it, careful not to disturb anything around Jill's body. Just like she did in Dr. B's office, Lacey felt for a pulse…and got the same result.

An intake of breath behind her stirred her hair, and a scream gathered in her lungs. Before the scream escaped her lips, a large hand clamped over her mouth, pressing the back of her head against a solid thigh.

She twisted her head and bit the hand that held her captive. The hand dropped, and she spun around on her knees, ready to launch out of the room when the intruder grabbed her arm.

"Lacey, it's me."

Her gaze flew to the stranger's face, only he wasn't a stranger at all. Dr. Perfect's perfect features were gathered in a scowl as he sucked on his hand.

"What the hell are you doing here?" She jumped up to face him. "Jill's dead, and you're creeping around her apartment?"

"Shhh." He gripped her shoulders, his fingers biting through her jacket into her flesh. "I'm not creeping around her apartment. I just got here."

"So your first instinct is to sneak up behind me and clap your hand over my mouth?" She wrenched out of his grasp. "Why are you here?"

"That's not important right now. What happened?"

"Isn't it obvious?" She spread her arms to encompass the disheveled bedroom. "The killer found Jill and murdered her, just like Dr. B, just like Debbie."

Rocking back, she covered her face as the enormity of the situation hit her square in the jaw. Nick engulfed her in an embrace, and her head fell all too easily against his shoulder. His arms tightened around her as he rested his chin on top of her head. He smelled like soap and toothpaste and comfort.

She rubbed her nose against his denim shirt, leaving a wet smudge, and looked up into his face. "We have to call the police."

"No!" His body stiffened. "Not yet."

"What's your problem?" She narrowed her eyes, pulling back from the reassurance of his arms. "At the very least, we have to get out of here. What if the killer comes back?"

"Let him try." Nick lifted his shirt to reveal a gun tucked into the waistband of his jeans.

"Have you lost your mind?" She stumbled back, her legs wedging against Jill's bed, all sense of comfort gobbled up by a wave of panic. "Why do you have a gun? Why are you even here?"

He closed his eyes and brushed a lock of dark hair back from his forehead. Blowing out a breath, he straightened his shoulders and looked her in the eyes.

"I'm here to save my brother's life."

Chapter Four

Confusion and mistrust mingled in Lacey's face. Her words about her father at lunch hinted at her low opinion of doctors. Nick had to work twice as hard to win her trust, and he knew instinctively the charm he tried diligently to cultivate for the phony life he led wouldn't do the job. Honesty and sincerity would win the day with Lacey Kirk, but he had very little of those qualities to share right now.

"What does your brother have to do with any of this?" She crossed her arms over her chest, as if creating a barrier to her heart, as if to guard her sympathy from phony sob stories.

He rubbed her unyielding shoulder, resisting an urge to take her in his arms again. It felt good having her there...too good. It had been years since he'd experienced any real emotion with a woman. He couldn't afford it ever since his brother went on the run. And even before that.

"Let's discuss this elsewhere." Although Lacey's feet seemed rooted to the carpet, Nick propelled her out of the bedroom and into Jill's Spartan living room. The woman lived as if ready to take flight at a moment's notice.

"Start discussing—" Lacey plucked a cell phone out of the purse hanging from her shoulder and smacked it against her palm "—because I'm about thirty seconds away from calling the cops."

Charm definitely wouldn't work with Lacey. He rubbed his chin. "My brother's the real target. Dr. Buonfoglio did some work on him. I think this killer is after the doctor's files to get information on my brother's changed identity and his whereabouts."

"I take it your brother isn't some actor who wants to keep his face-lift a secret, is he?" With her green eyes narrowed to slits, she resembled that cat washing itself in the bathroom.

"No." He planned to keep this short and simple.

"Why did Dr. B change your brother's face? Is your brother a bad person, a criminal?"

"He's made some bad choices, but he doesn't deserve to die for them. The people after him are worse."

"Does he owe them money?"

"Something like that." His brother's involvement with the De Luca Family went deeper than money, but the less she knew the better. He didn't want to explain how much he owed his brother, how his brother had saved his life and what it cost him to do it.

She turned and paced, but at least she no longer seemed poised for flight and she'd dropped the cell phone back in her purse.

He held his breath, waiting for the next question. Lacey had too much intelligence and integrity to accept his explanation at face value without further interrogation. He could almost hear her brain clicking as she worked through his story.

Hooking her thumbs in the pockets of her jeans, she stopped in front of him. "You're a cosmetic surgeon, why didn't your brother come to you?"

"He did come to me…for a referral. He didn't want to involve me." He'd begged T.J. to let him do the surgery, but his brother refused. Maybe T.J. knew the day would come when the De Lucas discovered he'd altered his face, and he didn't want his kid brother in the line of fire...even though T.J. had stepped into the line of fire for him.

"So you referred him to Dr. B? You dragged Dr. B into this mess?" She hunched her shoulders, her eyes shooting daggers at him. "You killed him."

Combing his hands through his hair, he sighed. He didn't want to get into all this. They didn't have time, but before he enlisted Lacey's help he had to convince her he deserved it.

"Lacey, Dr. B was already involved in this mess." He plucked her hand out of her pocket and rubbed his thumb in the center of her palm. "I referred my brother to Dr. Buonfoglio precisely because I knew he did that kind of work."

Her hand jerked in his. "Dr. B changed criminals' faces? Why? Why would he do something like that?"

"For Abby. He did it for Abby." He felt like scum playing the sympathy card, but he had to get through to her. One thing he'd discovered about Lacey Kirk was if she deemed you worthy, she'd brave the fires of hell to help you.

Shaking her head, she blinked her eyes. "What do you know about Dr. B's daughter?"

"I know it's expensive to keep her in that group home."

"Oh, my God, he did do it for the money."

"He did it for his daughter." He grabbed her other hand and pulled her toward him, a sharp pain lancing his chest. "A man will do just about anything for his child. Don't judge him, Lacey."

"In the end, how did Dr. B's criminal behavior help Abby? He's dead." Her mouth formed a thin, obstinate line.

She'd just appointed herself judge, jury and executioner, although someone else had handled that last job for her. She may have a boatload of sympathy, but she reserved it for those who earned it, like her patients. Could he earn her sympathy?

He squeezed her hands. "Look, we could debate this all night, but there's a dead woman in the bedroom and we have to call the cops."

"I'm glad you recognize that." She shrugged out of his grasp and reached into her purse for her cell phone.

He snatched the phone from her hand. "But first I'm asking for your help."

Her jaw hardened as she made a grab for her phone, but he held it above his head out of her reach.

"Who the hell do you think you are, Dr. Perfect?" Her brows snapped together, an angry flush rushing into her cheeks.

The phone almost slid from his grip. So that's what she thought of him. "That's just it, Lacey. I'm not perfect, and neither are you or Dr. B or anyone. Even if you won't help me, just give me a few minutes to search Jill's place."

"Search for what?" She waved her arms around the room. "The bad guys already did that, and if they found what they wanted, your brother's toast, anyway."

He dropped the phone, shoulders slumping under the heavy weight he'd been carrying more years than he cared to remember. Was he too late? Had the situation already slipped out of his control?

Lacey gasped and took his face in her hands. "Nick, I'm so sorry. What a stupid, insensitive thing to say, and I'm supposed to be the caring hospice nurse. If my teachers heard me, they'd cashier me right out of the program. I know all about hauling brothers who make bad choices out of trouble. Search away. Let me know when you're done, and we'll call the police. There's nothing anyone can do for Jill now, anyway."

And just like that, he got Lacey Kirk, crusader for justice, on his side without even trying. He kissed her mouth and pulled out a pair of rubber gloves from his pocket. He ignored her wide eyes, not bothering to determine if her shock came from the kiss or the gloves, and skirted the sofa to search through the papers on the floor.

He said over his shoulder, "This guy doesn't even know what he's looking for. It could be files, papers, a computer disk. Hell, I don't know what I'm looking for, either. If only Dr. Buonfoglio left some hint, some key about where he stashed information on these patients."

"A key!"

Nick twisted his head around. Lacey's face glowed with excitement, her eyes out-shining the Tiffany lamp. "Jill called me tonight. That's why I came over. She sounded distraught, then hysterical. She babbled on about a key. She wanted to give the key to me."

"That's it." Nick scrambled to his feet. "Where would she hide a key? The office?"

"I don't think it's at the office. She talked about giving me the key tonight. It must be here." She swallowed and looked down. "Unless the killer found it."

"He wouldn't understand the significance of a key unless Jill told him, and I don't think she did." He shook his head. "She knew he wouldn't spare her life even if she revealed everything."

Hands wedged on her hips, Lacey said, "Let's start looking. If we don't call the cops soon, the timeline of the murder will be all screwed up and raise some red flags."

Having Lacey on his side and in the know made his life easier, but how long would she stay on his side when she found out he had no intention of helping the police find this killer? He had his own way of dealing with the scumbag who'd murdered three people and turned Lacey's world upside down. And she didn't need to know about that.

"You look in here. I'll take the bedroom." He squeezed past her, a button on his shirt snagging the gold chain around her neck. She reached up and clasped the necklace in her hand. "I'm sorry. It didn't break, did it?"

"Nick." She ran her finger around the inside of the chain. "I remembered something else Jill said on the phone. She said she kept the key with her always."

"Yeah? Do you think it might be in her purse or something?"

"Always." She held her necklace out from her neck with one finger. "Jill always wore a silver chain with a heart. She has it on now."

"A heart?" He scratched the stubble on his chin. "A heart is not a key."

She grabbed his arm. "Will you look with me? I know a hospice nurse should be valiant in the face of death, but not this kind."

He took her arm and led her back into the bedroom. With his gloves still covering his hands, he leaned over Jill's lifeless body and drew the chain around her neck out from her blouse. A large silver heart dangled at the end of the chain.

"Look." Lacey's trembling finger zeroed in on the heart. "There's a hinge."

A pulse of excitement thrumming in his throat, Nick wedged his fingernail into the seam opposite the hinge and pried the heart open. Lacey gasped as a small silver key winked at them from the hollow space in the heart.

"Here's our key." He dabbed at it with the tip of his rubber glove, where it stuck, and examined it. Then he replaced it, snapped the locket shut, and removed it from Jill's mottled throat. "Now it's time to call the cops."

"You're not going to tell them about any of this, are you?"

He could almost see her digging the heels of her sneakers into the carpet. Tipping her chin up with his finger, he stared into her eyes. "I can't, Lacey. I have to protect my big brother."

"But the police won't turn your brother over to these people, will they? They can help him."

He had to trust that she wouldn't betray him, wouldn't allow her strong sense of justice to overrule the human element. He lifted a shoulder and dropped his hand from her face. "My brother, T.J., got involved with the wrong people, he ran a little gambling, laundered some money, but he turned important evidence over to the FBI, and even testified to put a bad guy behind bars. Then someone in the FBI compromised T.J.'s identity in the Witness Protection Program, and he can't trust anyone now…except me."

Groaning, she plowed her fingers through her hair. "This gets more and more complicated by the minute."

"And now it's urgent. The man T.J. testified against managed to get a retrial, and T.J. needs to come out of hiding to make sure he stays locked up."

She sucked in a breath. "The man's accomplices want to kill him before he gets another chance to testify?"

"Exactly. Please, Lacey, I have to protect my brother." He'd never been more sincere with a woman in his life, and it worked better than charm.

"Okay, let's discuss this later. We've wasted enough time, and if any witnesses saw us come in here we're going to have a lot of explaining to do."

He let out a long breath. "Nobody saw me, and there's no camera in the lobby. Hey, I'm a doctor, you're a nurse, so we can always say we tried to revive her first."

She pulled her cell phone out of her pocket and flipped it open. "What's your excuse for being here?"

"I was with you when Jill called. We came over together."

She raised one dark, sculpted brow. "You're a rather accomplished liar, Doc. Must come in handy juggling all those women."

He opened his mouth to protest, but she'd already punched in 911.

His reputation was worse than he'd thought.

THE KNOTS IN LACEY'S stomach loosened as Nick finally propelled her out of the lobby door and onto the sidewalk in front of Jill's apartment building. Red-and-blue lights from cop cars and an ambulance bathed the fog-shrouded street and the anxious faces of neighbors as they gathered in knots up and down the sidewalk.

Detective Chu had arrived, and he and the other officers were still combing through the crime scene.

Nick swung a cat carrier, containing Jill's orange tabby, at his side. Lacey insisted on taking the cat to save it from the animal shelter.

"I think that went well, don't you?" She stopped to button her jacket, ignoring the curious glances of the crowd. "Detective Chu didn't suspect anything unusual."

Nick turned to face her, the damp air curling the ends of his black hair and clinging to his long eyelashes. With his chiseled cheekbones and strong jaw, he was a walking advertisement for his cosmetic surgery practice. No wonder women fell at his feet. She widened her stance on the sidewalk to get a firm grip.

"I don't think Chu suspected us, but after three dead bodies he's damned curious about what this guy's after, and he's going to start digging," he said.

"Don't you think he's going to discover sooner or later that Dr. B had a hand in altering the faces of criminals? I mean, you knew that about him when you referred your brother to him."

As the heavy fog swirled between them, it created a curtain across Nick's face, obscuring his expression. "I had an inside track."

His words caused the butterflies in her stomach to beat their wings madly. She'd lied to the SFPD, a killer may be after her, and she was putting all her trust into this man with his dark good looks, silkily persuasive voice and shady past. She didn't know much more about him than she'd learned at lunch, except he had a criminal in his family.

She understood his need to protect his brother, but she couldn't allow this killer to get away with murdering Dr. B and his two nurses. It wasn't right. She scooped in a deep, salty breath. "Are you ever going to tell Detective Chu about your brother's involvement in this? About those files?"

"When my brother's safe. When I've destroyed those files." He glanced up at Jill's window, the light still burning. "Let's get going. I don't want Chu to discover us hanging around."

"Where's your car? We especially don't want Chu to see us leaving in different cars when we supposedly came here together."

He took her elbow and steered her across the street. "I took public transportation."

"I can give you a ride."

"You bet you are. I'm not letting you go home alone tonight."

Those butterflies made another trip around her insides, but this time fear didn't propel them. She groped for the keys in her purse. How had she succumbed to his charms so quickly? And he hadn't even turned on the charm. Two murder scenes hardly qualified as dinner and a movie, and she still felt zings of anticipation every time he touched her.

She unlocked the car door with her remote and he swung it open for her. "Move the front seat forward. I'll put Fifi in the back."

"You named her Fifi?"

He shrugged. "Do you know her name?"

"No, Jill never told me she had a cat." She flipped the front seat forward, so Nick could put the carrier in the backseat. "I came here just once and waited outside."

"Jill was a private person, huh?"

"I guess we know why." Lacey suppressed a shiver snaking up her spine. All three of her coworkers were in on the scam. Would the killer believe she was, too? Detective Chu told her to be careful, but the SFPD wasn't in the business of providing bodyguards or protective custody. She wasn't even a witness. She couldn't tell them much of anything about the masked killer.

Nick slammed the door, jogged around to the passenger side and slid into the car next to her. He smelled clean and soapy without the hint of the spicy, masculine cologne he usually wore. He'd replaced his customary suit with a pair of faded jeans and a loose denim shirt…that covered the gun in his waistband. The black stubble on his lean jaw gave him a dangerous look—more like Dr. Pirate than Dr. Perfect.

"Are you okay to drive?" He shot her a quizzical look and two dollops of heat scorched her cheeks. He must be an expert at reading women's responses, especially in the dark.

"Yes. I think I'm beyond shock right now." She started the car and glanced over her left shoulder before pulling onto the street. "What are you going to do with that key?"

"Just like Jill, I'm going to keep it with me. Somebody wants it, but he's going to have to kill me to get it."

She clutched the steering wheel. Judging from the determination of the killer, it might come to that. "What do you think it fits?"

"I don't know." He leaned into the backseat and tapped the cage in response to a squeak from the cat. "That's what we're going to try to find out tomorrow in Dr. Buonfoglio's office."

"We?" She echoed the cat's squeak. "Don't you have patients or something?"

He pointed to the bandage on his head. "I told my office I'm taking another day off to recover."

"They're going to find it mighty strange that you're taking time off in Dr. B's office, especially your nurse, Petra."

"Petra's a gossip."

"She'll probably spread it around that we're having a torrid affair."

"Would you mind?" His finger traced the line of her jaw.

Okay, now he *was* trying to charm her and she felt the full effect like a blast of heat from an open furnace. Time to put this man in his place. Just because she'd agreed not to rat him out to the cops didn't mean she'd fall prey to his seduction.

She flipped her hair back. "I suppose I'd rather have everyone think that than the truth."

Pinching her chin, he chuckled, a deep sound rumbling in the back of his throat. He pulled the locket from his pocket and pried it open. He held the key up, where it caught the light from street lamps and oncoming cars. "It's too small to fit a filing cabinet. Maybe a lockbox or wall safe. Could the good doctor be hiding a wall safe behind any pictures in the office?"

Thinking about the before-and-after photos in Dr. B's office and the bland landscapes in the waiting room, she wrinkled her nose. "Maybe, but more likely he'd keep something like that at home."

She jerked her head around at his quick intake of breath. His eyes glowed under raised brows.

"Oh, no, we don't." She shook her head to make sure he realized she meant it.

"Do you know where Dr. B lives?"

His house was ten minutes away, but Nick didn't have to know that. She waved her hand to the side. "Somewhere in North Beach."

She didn't fool him one bit.

"Come on, Lacey. What's the point of having the key if we can't find what it unlocks?"

"That's your problem. I just want the murderer to pay for what he did."

"So do I, and I'll tell Detective Chu everything once I destroy those files and ensure my brother's safety."

"You'll tell Chu everything?" She caught her breath. "You'll go to jail for obstruction of justice, interfering in a police investigation, and whatever else they can throw at you."

"I'm not a complete fool. I'll tell him I heard a rumor about Dr. Buonfoglio doing faces for criminals, and he can turn the info, minus my brother's file, over to the FBI."

She snorted. "Yeah, somehow I thought you'd protect yourself."

"I can't afford to go to jail. I have..." He swiped a hand across his face. "At least give me the address. Once we get to your place and make sure everything's okay there, I'll check out Dr. B's house on my own."

He trailed his fingertips along her arm, the light touch curling her toes. Is this how he persuaded women to rip off their clothes?

She sucked in her lower lip, feeling her resolve slip away in direct proportion to her curling toes. "You'd have an easier time of it if I searched with you. After all, I'm the one who knew about the key."

"I'd welcome your help, but I don't want you to get involved any more than you already have. Give me the address, and I'll make my own way over there."

She pulled a U-turn at the corner, pointing the car toward North Beach. "I'm in it up to my neck, Doc."

LACEY CIRCLED THE BLOCK once before squeezing into a parking space on the street. Was there nothing this woman didn't do well? He expected tears and hysterics at Jill's apartment, but Lacey handled herself...like a nurse.

He valued efficiency, order. Through order and efficiency, he'd kept a lid on the chaos that had characterized his early life. Now the madness threatened to explode, and he couldn't allow that to happen.

The tight reins he held on his emotions with an iron fist extended to dating. He favored superficial dates with superficial women. The fewer messy entanglements he had the better.

"Are you ready?" Lacey cut the engine and slipped the key out of the ignition. "I don't know how you think you're going to break into Dr. B's house in the middle of the night."

He slid a silver lock pick out of his back pocket and a flashlight out of his jacket and held them up. "The same way I planned to break into Jill's apartment."

Her eyes widened. "You're very resourceful. Must've learned all those skills from your brother."

He shrugged. Just because he let her in this far, didn't mean he had any intention of spilling the rest of his guts no matter how good it felt to have an ally.

"Do you think she's okay in here?" She jerked her thumb back at the cat.

"Are you suggesting we take a cat along on a break-in? She seems content wrapped up in that tight ball."

As she opened the car door, Lacey muttered, "She ain't the only one."

Was that a jab at his reticence? He hadn't been this open with a woman in, well, ever.

Nick followed Lacey's purposeful stride downhill on the sidewalk until they reached a gated house, tucked back from the street. For all her digs at his brother's criminal past, she adapted well to the lifestyle, as if she'd been born into it...like him.

"Wait." He grabbed her arm as she reached for the latch on

the black wrought-iron gate and yanked a pair of surgical gloves out of his pocket. "Put these on."

"Don't you need those, too?"

He dug into his pocket and dragged out a second pair. "I have a spare."

"Were you a Boy Scout?"

"Far from it." He snapped the gloves on and lifted the latch. The gate squeaked, and Nick slid his gaze to the left to make sure no pedestrians were heading down the side street. He pushed Lacey in front of him into the small yard, feeling a ripple along her back.

He put a gloved finger beneath her chin, the thin latex doing nothing to block the electric current he felt every time he touched her. "Are you sure you want to do this? You can wait in the car with Fifi."

"You need my help. Besides, I don't think Fifi likes me."

He ran a thumb across her lips, wondering how they'd taste if he gave her a proper kiss...or an improper one. He shelved that thought for another time.

"Let's try for a side door that's not so visible."

They crept around the side of the narrow house. The residence next to Dr. Buonfoglio's loomed so close, Nick could almost touch the walls of both houses with his arms spread wide. They approached a series of windows and Nick ducked, pulling Lacey down with him. They ran, crouching, to the back of the house.

Nick straightened and halted at the sight that greeted them. Lacey collided into his back.

"What are you doing?" she whispered, and the sound seemed amplified within the confines of the little patio.

Putting a finger to his lips, he pointed to the window, its screen off and resting against the side of the house. Lacey's face had a waxy glow in the moonlight, her eyes round with fear.

He wiggled his fingers into the open gap of the window and

pushed up the sash. The edge of a white curtain stirred in the breeze.

He put his lips close to her ear. "I'll go in first, and then help you inside."

"He's been here already." She clutched his arm. "He may still be here."

"My guess is he hit Dr. B's place before he even paid a visit to Jill, and don't forget…" He patted the comforting outline of the gun still shoved into his waistband.

She nodded, and he gripped the windowsill to hoist himself up.

"Hold on." Lacey dragged a cinder block from the side of the fence and wedged it against the house. "Use this."

He stepped on the block and eased into the house, dropping onto the floor next to an upended table. Looked as if they were following in the killer's footsteps.

He leaned out the window and hooked his arms beneath hers, dragging her through. Her foot lodged on the windowsill, and he jerked her body forward. She toppled against him, and they both fell to the floor.

His breath quickened, his arms tightening around her briefly before he pushed up from the floor, taking her with him.

"Sorry." He looked down into her flushed face and grinned.

Bending over, she brushed off her thighs, her hair creating a veil to hide her expression. "Sheesh, if the guy was still here, we'd both be dead by now."

Forty minutes later, after trying to insert the little key into every lock in the house and searching behind every picture on the wall, they stood in the middle of the living room exchanging frustrated glances.

Nick kicked the corner of the sofa with his toe. "There's nothing here."

"Unless the bad guy got to it first."

"We have the advantage, Lacey. At least we have the key."

"But we don't know what it unlocks."

"Maybe we'll have better luck at the office tomorrow." He brushed a cobweb off his jacket and sneezed.

A car engine rumbled outside, and Lacey stood to the side of the window and parted the curtain. She gasped and dropped the curtain. "It's the cops."

"Damn." He grabbed her hand and half dragged her to the back window, which still gaped open. He wrapped his hands around her waist and lifted her up, balancing her on the windowsill.

"Don't you dare push me out of this window," she hissed back at him.

He dropped his hands, and she scrambled outside. He then launched himself through and jammed the window down. He left the screen off, just the way they found it, and shoved the cinder block back to the fence.

"We can't go back out the way we came in. They'll see us." She twisted her hands in front of her, and guilt pricked the back of his neck for dragging her into this mess.

"Over the fence." He tapped the cinder block with his foot. She stepped onto it and clambered over the fence, dropping to the other side.

She called back over, "I sure hope these people don't have a pit bull."

He hopped over the fence to join her. "Me, too."

They climbed over another fence before slipping out to the sidewalk in the front. He dragged the gloves from his hands, nodding to her to do the same. A black-and-white, its radio crackling, was parked at the curb in front of Dr. Buonfoglio's house. A uniformed officer was talking to a woman in a bathrobe and curlers on the sidewalk, and they both looked down the street at Nick and Lacey.

Nick's heart bumped against his ribs, and he grabbed Lacey around the waist, turning her toward him. He lowered his lips to hers and kissed the gasp from her mouth. Her body went rigid and he deepened the kiss, his tongue darting along the seam of her lips.

She got it.

Melting against him, she returned the kiss, parting her lips in response to his insistent tongue. She tasted sweet and fresh and like everything he'd craved for so long.

With one hand planted firmly on the curve of her hip, he cupped the back of her head with his other, angling her mouth so he could explore its warmth. She rolled her hips forward, her thigh fitting neatly between his legs, pressing against his hardness. His fingers tangled in her silky hair as he devoured her mouth, drawing her closer still.

"Get a room," the woman in the bathrobe shouted down the street. "This isn't the Tenderloin."

Lacey jumped back from him, placing her palms against her cheeks.

He swallowed hard and managed a wink. "Good cover."

Slipping an arm around her shoulders, he guided her across the street to the car. With an unsteady hand, she pressed her remote to unlock the car. For good measure, he backed her up against the door, wedging his hands on either side of her shoulders. He kissed her hot, tasty lips again before lifting the door handle.

When he walked to the passenger side, he shot a glance at the cop and the neighbor. The other officer had come from the back of the house, and they were talking, ignoring him and Lacey.

Nick let out a breath and collapsed on the seat. "That was way too close for comfort."

"Yeah, way too close." She cranked on the engine. "How's Fifi doing back there?"

He craned his head over his shoulder. "Hasn't moved a whisker."

"Are you sure she's alive?"

He laughed. "I can see her breathing. She's probably stressed out."

"I can relate." Lacey drove past the cop car, carefully coming to a full stop at the stop sign and checking her rearview mirror.

"About that kiss—"

She cut him off. "Like you said, a good cover."

They drove in silence, and every once in a while Nick stole a glance at Lacey's profile. He couldn't read her thoughts, and it was a good thing she couldn't read his or she'd slap his face and dump him out at the next curb.

When they kissed on the street, he forgot where he was, forgot who he was. The ruse worked, but as soon as his lips met hers all pretense ended…for him, anyway.

He cleared his throat. "Where do you live?"

"Sunset. We're almost there."

The Sunset District lay inland from the Bay and didn't get as much fog as the rest of the city. It consisted of neat row houses, some mom-and-pop shops, and a sprinkling of funky restaurants. The area suited Lacey, but like any place in the city it boasted high-priced real estate. How'd she afford a house here on a nurse's salary unless she rented?

How was that any of his business?

She pulled up to the curb in front of a small house ringed by a low stone wall. A light glowed in the front window.

"Did you leave that light on?"

"Yeah, I did."

Before they got out of the car, Lacey reached for the cat carrier. Nick placed a hand on her arm. "Let's check things out first."

Nodding, she swallowed hard.

Nick took Lacey's arm as they approached the silent house.

Jasmine vines crept along the wall, filling the air with their sweet, intoxicating scent. When they reached her porch, Nick slid the gun from his waistband.

"You're awfully fond of waving that thing around."

"It's not going to do any good stuffed in my pants."

"I'm glad there's nobody around to overhear this conversation. They might get the wrong idea." She pressed a hand against her mouth, stifling a giggle.

Looked like he wasn't the only one whose thoughts were hovering below the belt since that hot kiss.

He put a finger to his lips. "Let's hope there's nobody around."

Her giggle ended in a choking sound. As she widened her eyes in fear, he silently cursed himself for bringing her back to reality.

She unlocked the dead bolt, and then slid her key in the door-handle lock, pushing the door open. He held her back and stepped across the threshold first. The warmth of her house enveloped him. The fragrance of scented candles mingled with the mouth-watering aroma of spicy, home-cooked food. Her hodgepodge of furniture created a colorful setting that invited visitors to sink onto the overstuffed sofa and kick up their feet on the mismatched ottoman.

But they didn't have time to relax.

"Was he here?" She pushed past him and stood in the center of the room, hands on her hips. "I don't see anything out of order."

"Stay here." He removed the safety from his gun and gripped it in one hand as he stalked across the living room toward the hallway.

He pushed open a door, his gaze immediately drawn to Lacey's dresser drawers, gaping open and frothing over with underwear.

But before he could admire her taste in lingerie, her blood-chilling scream echoed down the hallway.

Chapter Five

The eyes stared at her from the bathroom mirror over the sink—two circles with dots in the center—just like the note on her windshield.

Her throat felt raw. Had she screamed?

She braced her hands against the doorjamb to keep from sliding to the floor. Nick came up behind her, the warmth from his body soaking into her stiff back. Suddenly the kindhearted nurse who supported everyone else needed someone to lean on, and she didn't even care that the nearest candidate had a reputation as a player and a cad.

She collapsed against Nick's chest, and his arms wrapped around her, his gun dangling toward the floor. His warm breath stirred her hair as he whispered, "Lock yourself in the bathroom. I'm going to check the rest of the house."

"I don't want to be alone in here with…that." She twisted in his arms to face him. The hard line of his jaw and the dangerous glint in his eyes reassured her. She didn't know how or why, but with the click of a gun the suave Dr. Perfect could morph into a tough guy no one would want to cross in a dark alley.

"Okay, come with me." He brushed a lock of hair from her cheek. "Keep behind me and follow closely."

She'd follow him anywhere, anytime. He turned, the gun

leveled in front of him, and she hooked her finger in the belt loop of his jeans under his jacket. She didn't plan to allow this man out of her reach.

They searched the remaining two bedrooms and the kitchen, discovering the intruder's mode of access when broken glass from the window in her little dining area crunched beneath their feet. They threw open closets and flooded the garage with light. The killer was gone, but he'd left ransacked desks, drawers and filing cabinets in his wake.

Still gripping Nick's belt loop with cramped fingers, Lacey followed him into the hallway. He stopped between her bedroom and the bathroom, and her forehead banged into his back.

"Sorry," she mumbled into his jacket.

"You can let go now."

Could she? He represented her lifeline in this nightmare. If she let go would he desert her? Leave her to handle the crisis on her own? Not that she couldn't handle it. She'd always managed before, and she could do it again. She dragged in a ragged breath and released her hold on him.

Nick reached back and grabbed her hand, pulling her to his side. Curling an arm around her waist, he asked, "How are you doing?"

"I—I'm fine." She hated the tremor in her voice and straightened her shoulders to counter it.

"No, you're not." He swept her into his arms and balanced his chin on top of her head.

She allowed her shoulders to slump as she melted against his strong body. Just for this moment she'd give in to the weakness born by fear, and succumb to the good doctor's ministrations.

His long fingers massaged the back of her neck and then kneaded the tight knot between her shoulder blades. She closed her eyes as he stroked her throat, and her tension seeped away.

A feather-light touch trailed along her jaw, and she pulled back from Nick's arms. As much as she wanted to stay right here in his comforting embrace, the terror that threatened them still loomed in the shadows. Even Nick's soothing touch couldn't blot out the fact that the killer would strike again, and she had a target painted on her back as long as he believed she had information about Dr. B's practice.

"Nick, we have to call the cops, Detective Chu." She stopped. The mess in her bedroom caught her eye and she gasped. "Oh, my God, he went through my things, my underwear."

A white-hot anger blinded her as she stumbled into her room and sank to her knees before the tousled dresser. Her hands trembled as she shoved satin straps and silky lace into the drawers.

"This is horrible. I feel so violated. What did he hope to find in here?"

Crouching beside her, Nick scooped up some lingerie from the floor and handed it to her, placing other items in the open drawer.

The sight of his strong hands lingering in the folds of her lacy bras and panties sent heat of another kind spiraling to her belly.

"That's all right. I'll do this." She shooed his hands away.

He pushed up from the floor and retreated to the doorway. "I'm sorry, Lacey."

"No problem." A warm flush ebbed into her cheeks when she realized she was waving a pair of polka-dot bikini panties at him. She stuffed the panties in the drawer and slammed it shut. "I probably shouldn't even be putting this stuff away before the cops get here."

"I meant, I'm sorry you're in the middle of my nightmare."

"It's not your fault, Nick. Dr. B dragged me into this when he hired me, and Jill dragged me in further when she called and babbled about a key."

She closed the remaining dresser drawers and jumped to her feet. "Now I suppose it's time to call the cops."

"You can't call the cops, Lacey." Nick stood at the entrance to her bedroom, arms folded, his broad shoulders almost spanning the width of the doorway.

"What are you talking about?" He was taking this whole obstruction-of-justice thing a little too far. The police had a right to know about this most recent break-in. "The guy broke in to my house. He knows where I live. H-he ransacked my underwear for God's sake. He's gotta pay."

"He's going to pay. I'll make him pay, but we can't let the police in on everything. I told you, the FBI will want to talk to my brother, and I can't allow that. I have to keep the cops off the trail for a little while longer."

"Why are you protecting a criminal? Even the Uni-bomber's brother turned him in."

Pinching the bridge of his nose, Nick squeezed his eyes shut. He suddenly looked older, tired and not so perfect.

"My brother's no bomber, and I owe him. He saved my life…once."

"And it sounds like he's been making it hell ever since." She dug her hands into her hips, but she'd already conceded defeat and she had a feeling he wasn't about to tell the story of how his criminal brother had saved him.

Wouldn't be much point in telling the cops or Detective Chu about this latest break-in, anyway. They wouldn't find any evidence in her upended house, and they already told her they couldn't offer her any protection. Her gaze slid to Nick's tense face. Could he?

"Please, Lacey, trust me. I won't let anything happen to you."

Trust him? Didn't seem she had any other choice right now. She exhaled. "Okay."

His shoulders relaxed and he shoved off the door. "Pack a bag."

"What?" Time for the next dip on the roller coaster. "Why am I packing a bag?"

"You can't stay here. That's obvious. He knows where you live, and he'll come for you."

Goose bumps rushed up her arms, and she hugged herself. She'd tried to push that thought away, but the truth of it chilled her to the core.

Once again Dr. Nick came to the rescue as he wrapped his arms around her. She inhaled his comforting scent, not expensive cologne and even more expensive fabric, but pure, potent masculinity. The smell made her feel safe and protected...and incredibly aroused.

She wanted to go home with him. She wanted to know what it felt like for this man to take control of her body the way he'd taken control of her mind and actions over the past five hours. She'd done things that would've been unthinkable for her only hours ago. Would Nick have the same effect on her in bed?

"I'm sorry." He stroked her hair. "I didn't mean to put it so bluntly, but you're not safe here."

But she'd be safe with him...in his home, in his bed. Nestling her head against his solid chest, she almost purred, feeling pity for that poor, abandoned cat in the car.

"We'll get you checked into a hotel tonight under an assumed name."

At his words, like a dash of cold water on her face, she jerked her head up. At least the cat got to go home with him.

"Don't worry." He patted her shoulder. "I'll pay for it."

She placed her palms against that rock-hard chest and shoved. "I don't need your money. I can pay for a hotel."

He blinked his spiky, dark lashes. "I know you can, but I feel responsible for your predicament. Let me take care of it."

How many times had she cautioned herself not to fall under Dr. Perfect's seductive spell? Before this mess started, she'd worked overtime to keep out of his way. She'd heard the stories.

He used people. She'd help him out because the sooner they found the files and destroyed them, the sooner she'd get her life back. But she'd be on her guard. She'd been putty in his deft surgeon's hands, but she knew his touchy-feely tricks now.

And as long as he was using her, she'd use him right back.

She shrugged. "Okay, you can pay for the hotel and all my food. Knock yourself out."

He raised an eyebrow and bowed at the waist. "At your service. Throw some clothes in a bag, and let's get out of here."

She pulled open the door of the hall closet and gasped. Nick appeared at her side in an instant, worry creasing his face.

"What's wrong?"

"The cat. The hotel won't allow a cat."

His brows snapped together. "Is that all? I'll take the thing home."

"You're going to take care of a cat?" She struggled with her suitcase, and Nick crouched next to her and yanked her bag out of the closet.

He lifted a shoulder. "I have someone who can take care of her."

Yeah, he probably employed housekeepers, cooks and gardeners.

Lacey darted between her bedroom and bathroom, tossing clothes and toiletries in a suitcase. She shot a glance at Nick, hunched over her books and notes from class. He really didn't have to feign interest in her life anymore. He had her right where he wanted her...wrapped firmly around his scalpel-wielding fingers…from the moment he charged into Dr. B's office on his white horse.

But only in regards to this search. She'd help him comb through the office tomorrow, and then he was on his own. She'd stay in the hotel, with his compliments, stay away from the hospital, and stay away from him.

She dropped the bag by the door and dug her keys out of her purse. "Ready?"

"This is interesting stuff." He looked up from the kitchen table. "You use a lot of psychology in the program, a lot of ideas from Eastern medicine and philosophy."

"We encourage our patients to meditate, to view death as another journey. The nurses use it, too…to cope with the loss of our patients."

"How do you do it?" He snapped the book closed. "I don't think I could handle watching my patients die week after week, month after month."

"It's all about the preparation." She couldn't explain her selfish motivations to Nick. She couldn't tell him that every desertion, the death of each patient, only made her stronger. When her father abandoned his family for a new-and-improved model, it hurt like hell. She'd crumbled inside but never showed it. With each subsequent loss, she crumbled a little less.

"Are you taking your books with you?"

"No, I have a short break before my next class starts, and I can always come back for them, right?"

"Sure. Let me walk out first. Give me your keys."

He unlocked her car door and jogged down the street to peer into a couple of parked cars. Then he returned and escorted her to the car.

"How's Fifi?"

He twisted into the backseat, reaching toward the cage. "She's fine. I'll give her some food and water when I get home."

"Where's home?"

"Pacific Heights."

She snorted and cranked on the engine.

"Do you have something against money?" He pulled the gun out of his waistband and settled it on the floor of her car.

"If I say yes, will you shoot me?"

He laughed. "No, I'm just curious. Money means security and power. It isn't inherently evil, although some means of acquiring it are. Speaking of money, you're staying at the Grand Marquis in Nob Hill."

She whistled and smacked the thighs of her faded jeans. "Maybe I should change first."

"So you're familiar with the Grand Marquis? It's a good place because it's big, crowded and busy. You'll never be alone there." He turned to look out the back, then powered down his window to manually adjust the side view mirror. "Nobody's following us, but if I notice anything suspicious I'll give you an alternate route."

She nodded and merged with a line of traffic heading north. Okay, maybe she expected too much from him. Why should he invite her to camp out at his place? He had a life outside of all this cloak-and-dagger stuff, maybe he even had the girlfriend du jour sleeping at his place. That thought felt like bamboo shoots under her fingernails.

She skimmed a hand through her hair, pushing it off her face. "I used to live in Nob Hill—big sprawling house with a view— and I know firsthand money can cause all sorts of problems."

Nick drew in a sharp breath, and she braced her palms against the steering wheel. *Here it comes.*

"Is your father Bradley Kirk, the world-renowned heart surgeon?"

"Guilty." She threw up her hands. "But if you're hoping for an introduction or an opportunity to kiss his ring, I can't help you. He's semiretired and plying his trade in Florida, and I rarely see him."

"I don't kiss anybody's ring."

The hard edge to his voice caused her to snap her head around to stare at his profile in the darkened car. It looked as if it was carved from granite. Must've hit a nerve, which further cemented her belief that all doctors had a God complex. Of course Nick didn't want to kiss anybody else's ring. Only he deserved that honor.

They drove in silence, broken occasionally by Nick's instructions to turn a corner or pull over for a few minutes until he could be satisfied that the car behind them didn't pose a threat.

By the time Lacey pulled up to the glittering facade of the Grand Marquis, her nerves were tighter than a new face on one of Dr. Nick's patients.

She released the trunk, and Nick jumped from the car to pluck the parking ticket from the valet's outstretched hand. Nick then pulled her suitcase from the trunk and dropped it on the ground.

"If they take my car, how are you going to get home?"

"I'll take a taxi." He flipped the front seat forward and lifted Fifi's cage from the car. The cat opened one eye and sighed.

"She looks stuffed." She still couldn't imagine Nick with a cat. It was a good thing Jill had an old, nearly comatose one instead of a lively kitten.

"I'm sorry, sir. The Grand Marquis doesn't allow pets." The parking attendant pointed an accusing finger at Fifi.

"I'm not staying." Nick pulled out the handle of her suitcase and wheeled it toward the entrance, where the doorman opened the door while keeping a wary eye on the cat carrier.

Lacey followed Nick as he marched through the lobby, defiantly wheeling her suitcase and swinging the cat carrier at his side. She shoved her hands in the pockets of her scruffy blue jeans, glancing left and right at the well-dressed, well-heeled guests mingling in the lobby and descending the sweeping staircase in evening wear. Just her luck. The hotel seemed to be hosting some glittering affair.

Nick's appearance wasn't much better than hers—his jeans sported plenty of dirt and a rip in the thigh courtesy of one of those fences they'd hopped. But he carried himself as if he owned the joint, and the clerk at the front desk snapped to attention when he planted himself at the counter.

In a matter of minutes, the female clerk gushed and fluttered and addressed him as "Dr. Marino," as in "Of course, Dr. Marino" or "Anything you say, Dr. Marino."

He looked over his shoulder. "All they have available is a suite. Is that okay?"

A suite at the Grand Marquis? That was more than okay. That was pure decadence. And if she had to live her life in fear of a methodical, relentless killer, she might as well do it in style.

"That's fine." She joined him at the counter, leaning against its edge.

The hotel clerk looked up and smiled. "I'm sure your sister will be quite comfortable, Dr. Marino."

Sister? She clenched her jaw, grinding her teeth. He could've at least pretended he'd brought her here for sinfully naughty purposes. Tugging at the hem of her sweatshirt, she scuffed the toe of her sneaker against the polished floor. Okay, maybe not dressed like this.

Nick finished the transaction with the eyelash-batting clerk and snapped his fingers for the bellhop, who rushed over as if his job depended on it.

"I'll bring this right up, Dr. Marino." The bellhop snatched the suitcase and hovered over the cat. "This, too?"

"No, I'm taking the cat with me. You can take my sister up to her room now."

Lacey pursed her lips. How the hell did the bellhop know Nick's name, and why was he willing to take a cat to her room?

Taking her arm, Nick pulled her away from the bellhop. "Be careful. Watch your surroundings. I'll meet you at Dr. B's office tomorrow morning at nine, and we can start searching."

"Are you a frequent guest here?" She pulled away from him and crossed her arms.

"They know me." He quirked an eyebrow. "And it's a good thing they do, or you wouldn't have gotten a room tonight, Cindy Marino."

He probably brought women here, lots of women. And she didn't know what twisted the knife in her gut more—that he'd brought her to a place where he had romantic trysts…or that he hadn't brought her here for the same purpose.

She scowled and whipped up a quick retort, but before she could lash him with it, he leaned over and landed a hard kiss on her mouth. Gulping the retort, she watched his tall frame negotiate the revolving doors with Fifi's cage clutched at his side.

She turned to the bellhop, his mouth wide open enough to catch several flies at once, and swept past him to the elevator.

"My brother is very affectionate."

Chapter Six

Nick pulled his BMW into his reserved parking space after taking a circuitous route to his office building. Looked like the killer didn't have him on his radar…yet.

If the guy did see him with Lacey, he might wonder at their association. Nick didn't want to risk anyone linking him to Dr. Buonfoglio and his murder, but he didn't want to hang Lacey out to dry on her own, either. If the De Luca family got suspicious and investigated Dr. Nick Marino, he'd open himself, and those he loved, to a world of pain.

He'd have to pretend a personal rather than a professional connection to Lacey. That wouldn't be hard to do, although he'd have a helluva time convincing her to play along. She obviously loathed his lifestyle and misread the situation at the Grand Marquis last night.

Did she really think he brought women to the Marquis for lusty assignations? The idea seemed to piss her off. He punched the elevator button with a smile tugging at the corner of his mouth.

Or maybe his introduction of her as his sister was what pissed her off.

Before entering his own office, he glanced down the hall

toward Dr. Buonfoglio's office. Yellow tape still criss-crossed the doorway, but the SFPD hadn't sent a uniform today.

His receptionist, Zoe, looked up as he pushed through the doorway.

"Good morning, Dr. Marino. We didn't expect you today."

"Good morning. I'm here to check messages, and then I'm going to help Lacey Kirk with a few details regarding Dr. Buonfoglio's patients."

Zoe raised her brows and shot a sideways glance at Petra, hovering behind her. "Are we taking all of his patients?"

"No, but I'm going to help Lacey with referrals."

Petra and Zoe exchanged looks and started whispering as he sailed past them to his office. Good. Let them think he had a thing for Lacey. They wouldn't be far from the truth, anyway.

He settled behind his desk and flipped through a stack of messages, pulling out the ones he had to answer. He'd built a thriving practice, innovated a few revolutionary cosmetic surgery techniques, and was a regular on the lecture and convention circuit. It afforded him the time and money to do the work that brought him real satisfaction—performing surgeries for the kids in burn units and traveling to war-torn countries to repair the damaging effects of shrapnel from car bombs.

He refused to keep a low profile. He owed it to his brother to live it up, enjoy the lifestyle T.J. had to sacrifice.

Zoe stuck her head in the doorway, her face white. "Detective Chu is here to see you. H-he said Jill Zombrotto was murdered last night, and you were there."

"Unfortunately, that's true." Nick gripped the pen on his desk. Had Chu discovered something, some link between him and the murderer? "I was with Lacey when Jill called her. By the time we got there, Jill was dead."

Zoe's eyes widened, and she gulped. "So that's both Jill

and Debbie. Lacey must be terrified. Are the cops doing anything to protect her?"

They might be if he'd been honest with them. Nick stuffed down his guilt about lying to the police along with his guilt over leaving Lacey in a hotel by herself. He knew she'd be safe if she stayed put at the Marquis, but she'd be safer with him, at his house. He just couldn't allow that. Not now.

Shrugging, he pushed back from his desk. "The cops can't do anything. She's not exactly a witness, and she's not in imminent danger."

"Yeah, the cops don't want you to call them unless someone's breaking through your window with a knife." She shook her head. "So should I send Detective Chu in here? He has another guy with him."

"Of course." Nick stood up, his pulse thrumming. This other guy had better not be FBI. The fibbies would have an easier time discovering the true identity of Dr. Nick Marino than would the SFPD.

Detective Chu, stylish in his Hugo Boss suit, entered Nick's office followed by a burly man in a wrinkled trench coat.

"Good to see you again, Dr. Marino." Chu stuck out his hand and gestured to the big man by the door. "This is my partner, Detective Pratt."

Nick allowed his pent-up breath to seep out of his nose as he sized up Pratt. He invited the two men to sit down and got ready to lie.

"Did you turn up anything in Jill's apartment after we left, Detective Chu?"

"As a matter of fact, we did. Jill's neck had the distinct markings of a chain or some kind of necklace. When the killer strangled her, he must've pressed this necklace against her throat, leaving the impression of the chain."

Wrinkling his brow, Nick steepled his fingers. "A necklace?"

"Yes, but we never found any necklace, only its imprint on her throat." Chu flipped open a notebook, which had lain un-attended on his lap.

"Maybe it broke when he strangled her and he took it with him." Nick laced his fingers and rested his chin on top of his hands. He remembered the necklace sticking to Jill's throat and should've realized the cops wouldn't miss that. Wouldn't Chu and Pratt be interested to know that the necklace, with the key nestled inside, rested in the inside pocket of the jacket hanging on the back of his door.

After a few more questions that led nowhere, the detectives stood up to leave.

"Can you do anything to protect Lacey?" Nick rose behind his desk, clutching the edge.

Chu tucked his glasses in his pocket. "The SFPD isn't in the business of providing bodyguards, Dr. Marino. She needs to be careful and report anything suspicious to us, but until this guy makes his move, there's not much we can do. Is there someone she can stay with?"

"She checked into a hotel last night."

Chu turned at the door. "What's your interest in Lacey Kirk? Why were the two of you together last night?"

"She's an attractive woman, Detective." Nick lifted a shoulder and pasted on his best devilish grin. "And I like attractive women."

Chu shook his head. "She's an attractive woman with a brand-new accessory—a target on her back."

LACEY STEPPED OFF THE elevator and rounded the corner. She gasped and backpedaled. Detective Chu and another cop-type were leaving Nick's office. They could forget about getting anything out of Nick. Beneath that glossy exterior, the man was wound tighter than a spool of thread.

She didn't even want them to try to get anything out of her. If Nick was a spool of thread, she more closely resembled an old ball of yarn. They could look at her sideways and she'd unravel.

She grabbed the door handle of the nearest office and stumbled inside. The receptionist glanced up with raised brows.

Lacey held the door open a crack and peered into the hallway, flattening herself against the wall. The detectives stopped in front of the elevator.

The receptionist cleared her throat. "Can I help you with something?"

"I think I have the wrong day for my appointment." Lacey looked over her shoulder, and then turned back to the door when she heard the elevator doors open.

"*Your* appointment?"

"Yeah, Cindy Marino. Can you check for me, please?"

The men stepped into the elevator, and Lacey exhaled. Dodged 'em. She was pretty good at this cloak-and-dagger stuff.

"Uh, Dr. Carson is a pediatrician. You couldn't possibly have an appointment with her."

Lacey's cheeks burned. Maybe not so good at the cloak-and-dagger stuff, after all. "Sorry, looks like I have the wrong day *and* the wrong doctor."

She shoved the door open and stepped into the empty hallway. The receptionist called after her, "Aren't you Lacey Kirk, Dr. Buonfoglio's office manager?"

Looked like she totally sucked at this cloak-and-dagger stuff.

Yellow tape barred the entrance to Dr. B's office. Lacey unlocked the door and ducked under the tape.

"Wait for me."

Nick, face flushed, stopped the door from closing with one well-shod foot. He was decked out in another designer suit today. The man could grace the cover of the special doctors' edition of *GQ*, if they had a special doctors' edition.

He followed her and snapped the door closed. "How'd you sleep last night? Everything okay at the hotel?"

"Just peachy. I needed a few glasses of wine after all the excitement, and what's wine without cheese? So I had some nice Brie and crackers sent up along with the wine. I put it on my brother's tab."

"Your brother's a generous guy."

"And a bit of a pervert." She folded her arms to signal a disapproval she didn't feel. "You should've seen the bellhop's eyes after that kiss."

"Guess I slipped out of character." He placed a finger beneath her chin, tilting her head up. "I couldn't help myself."

Her gaze dropped to his sensuous lips, now curved into a smile. She stepped back. Oh, no. They had a job to do, and then she'd extricate herself from his tangled web. A criminal for a brother. Lying to the police. Crooked FBI agents. A different woman every week. His life spelled chaos with a capital C.

Ever since Mom's illness, Dad's desertion and her brother Ryan's foray to the dark side, Lacey prized order. She took control of everything and everyone, even her patients. She wouldn't allow Dr. Nick Marino with his perfect features and imperfect life to charge in and spoil all that.

"We'd better get to work." She waved her arms around the waiting room. "I'll start looking in here. Can you take Dr. B's office?"

She couldn't face that bloodstain on the carpet, but Nick didn't need to know that. He had no problem keeping her in the dark about much more important issues. She sensed he'd held back when he clued her in on his brother's situation.

How did one brother wind up a cosmetic surgeon, and the other a criminal? Where were his parents? Why did he conveniently locate his office in the same building and on the same floor as the doctor who cut his brother's face?

And why was he a serial dater?

"I'd be happy to search Dr. B's office." He squeezed her shoulder as he brushed past her. "I know it's probably hard for you to go in there."

She sucked in her breath as she watched his tall form disappear into the back. So much for keeping secrets from Nick. And so much for disentangling herself from the silky strands he twined around her heart without even trying.

She got to work, shifting pictures on the wall to search behind them, and moving furniture in the unlikely event Dr. B hid a safe or a filing cabinet there.

After fifteen minutes of fruitless searching, she sat back on her heels and blew a wisp of hair from her face. "Are you having any better luck in his office?"

He called out, "No, how about around your desk?"

Stretching, she muttered, "I think I know what's in my own desk."

"What?"

"Nothing," she called back as she pushed through the swinging partition to her work space. She unlocked her desk and rummaged through each drawer, stopping at the one where she had kept Dr. B's appointment book…the stolen one.

Maybe those special appointments highlighted in blue held some clue to the patients, something she'd missed before, not that Nick's brother would be in the appointment book. He must've had his surgery a number of years ago. Three years ago? Is that why Nick moved into this building and onto this floor?

She and Nick met in the hallway, and he shrugged. "Nothing behind any of the pictures or diplomas in his office. I checked the rifled filing cabinet, but the key doesn't fit, anyway. I can't believe he doesn't have a computer on his desk."

"Dr. B was low-tech. I can go through my computer files, but I'm certain there's nothing there. I'm going to print out the year's appointments, which match the appointment book the guy stole. There might be something I missed."

"You do that, and I'll search behind the rest of the pictures. I'm sure this key fits a wall safe." Nick had removed his suit jacket and now unbuttoned his cuffs. He shoved the sleeves up to his elbows, revealing the corded muscles of his forearms. Strong, capable arms.

"Oh, I forgot." He returned to Dr. B's office and emerged clutching a black notebook. "This looks like Dr. Buonfoglio's personal calendar. I thumbed through it, but he used a lot of shorthand, which I can't understand. You'll probably have an easier time deciphering his notes than I will."

"I'll take a look." She placed it next to her computer and then logged in. "We won't have many more opportunities to look around this office, since Dr. B's daughter is coming out from New Jersey in a few days to settle his practice and pack up."

Nick gave a muffled response from somewhere in the back, and Lacey shrugged as she opened her first file. Nothing she looked into pertained to Dr. B's top-secret patients. He never gave her access to that information, and during the time she worked here she never found that odd. But the more she thought about it, the more the puzzle pieces fell into place.

She could understand it if he secured those files in a locked cabinet in the office, but to keep them in some hush-hush location with Jill wearing the key around her neck at all times? It only made sense if those patients feared loss of life, not loss of vanity.

She opened the database containing the appointments. She'd highlighted the special appointments in blue on the online version, as well. She clicked the print button and continued looking into other files and copying some of them to a CD.

An hour later, Nick perched on the edge of her desk with

a smudge of dirt on his chin and his black hair ruffled. "I couldn't find a damn thing."

"Ditto." She ejected the CD and logged off the computer. She scooped the appointment pages from the printer tray and stacked them on top of Dr. B's personal calendar, winding a rubber band around both. "Now what?"

"If we can't find my brother's files, they sure as hell can't find them. My brother has about a week and a half until he comes out of hiding to testify. If his identity remains a secret until then, he's home free. Once he testifies against the man on trial and fingers the bad apples in the FBI, he can get resettled."

"You have some dirt on your face." She plucked a tissue from the box on her desk and dabbed at the spot on his chin as his eyes darkened.

A muscle twitched in his jaw, but he allowed her to wipe away the smudge. She managed to smear the spot even more, and his intense gaze burning into hers didn't help matters. She dropped the tissue into the trash can.

He cleared his throat and shifted on the desk. "I just have to hope the people after him will be as unsuccessful as we've been in locating those files. They're on a deadline. Once my brother testifies, the FBI can safely relocate him."

"How does he know about the corruption in the FBI?"

"They used him." He dragged his fingers through his hair. "Once he gave them the information they wanted, they placed him in the Witness Protection Program, but they failed to protect him. They gave up his new identity and whereabouts to the De Luca family in exchange for other, better information."

"The De Luca family?" Her stomach dipped and she clutched her arms around her waist. "You told me he owed some people money."

"I'm sure he does, but he also ratted out a member of the De Luca family."

"So the FBI is working with the De Lucas? I thought this kind of thing belonged in a conspiracy theorist's fantasy world."

"It's not the entire FBI. The betrayal of my brother involved a few agents. Problem is, my brother doesn't know which ones. He won't know until he reveals names, dates and numbers, but he's not going to do that until he testifies."

She clasped her hands between her knees. "Okay, just whose trial is this, anyway?"

"Big Jimmy De Luca's."

"Your brother is testifying against Jimmy De Luca?"

"Unfortunately for him."

"Oh, my God, Nick." She stepped back, hitting her chair. It wheeled backward, crashing into her desk. "Your brother's in the mob."

"Not exactly. He did some work for them, but didn't realize he was dealing with the De Lucas."

"Oh, please. Once you're involved with the mob, they never let you out. I watched *The Sopranos*." She clapped her hands over her mouth. "Will they come after you? Do they know you're T.J.'s brother?"

"I've taken steps to prevent that." He grasped her wrists, pulling her hands away from her face. "They've been looking for my brother ever since they found out he planned to testify again. They haven't found him yet, and they haven't found me yet."

"Yeah, but they did find his cosmetic surgeon. Why didn't Dr. B give up the info to save his own life?"

"I hate to burst your bubble, but Dr. Buonfoglio didn't just work on my brother, Lacey. He made a regular practice out of altering faces for criminals. I'm sure he figured if he gave up those files, he'd be a dead man, anyway, because his former patients would come after him. He was playing a dangerous game."

"And Debbie and Jill?"

"They were playing the same game. Once the police start digging deeper, they'll find all kinds of secret bank accounts." He dropped her hands. "I found some papers at Jill's apartment last night that contained a list of several offshore accounts."

She looked into his dark, unfathomable eyes with the lids half mast. "Did you take them?"

"Of course. I don't want the police to figure this out just yet."

"This is crazy, Nick." She turned away from him and his dark, dangerous allure. What happened to the playboy doctor? The shallow, money-obsessed womanizer? Why couldn't she have that Dr. Nick Marino? The simple one. "I—I can't do this anymore. I don't want to be involved."

He stroked the back of her hair, and she almost melted in a puddle at his feet, ready to give him anything.

"I know. You've done enough, more than enough, and I'm sorry you got sucked into this." His hand slid to her waist, and he pulled her around. "But even without the junk I dumped in your lap, you're involved because you worked in this office. You still need to be careful. This can all be over in less than two weeks. They won't care after my brother spills his guts on the witness stand."

"What now?"

"Stay at the hotel. The police can't offer any protection other than sending a few squad cars to your house, but I'll check on you and I know most of the security guards at the hotel. They'll keep an eye on you. And watch your back."

That last bit of advice made the hair on the back of her neck quiver. *Yeah, just your regular day in the city.*

"I was supposed to attend a fund-raiser tonight, but I'll hang out at the hotel with you instead." He stood up and shook down his sleeves. "I'll walk you to your car and follow you out, and remember we were in here going over patient records for referrals."

Of course. What else would Dr. Perfect be doing with her?

"You don't have to cancel your appearance at the fund-raiser on my account. I'm safe enough at the hotel. Go, mingle, raise money for younger faces and bigger breasts. You can walk me out, but I have to use the ladies' room first."

"You head back to the hotel, and I'll be there later." He grabbed his jacket from the back of a chair. "I'll meet you in the hallway. I have to check in at my office."

Lacey locked up Dr. B's office. She'd have to turn her keys over to his daughter when she arrived. Nick slipped into his office and she continued down the hallway to the ladies' room.

Would she even see Nick after this was all over? Probably around the hospital while his legions of adoring fans trailed him. She snorted. Little did they know they idolized a criminal, or at least a scofflaw. No, a scofflaw parked in the handicapped parking zone. Nick impeded a police investigation and tampered with evidence. And so did she.

She pushed out of the stall and washed her hands. She jumped when the bathroom door swung open, then relaxed when Petra, eyes shining with curiosity, sidled up next to her at the vanity.

"So what were you and Dr. Marino doing in there all afternoon?" She snatched a tissue from the dispenser and patted her lips, but she didn't fool Lacey. She must've rushed in here the minute Nick went back to his office.

"I told you before. Dr. Marino's helping with the referrals for Dr. B's patients." She reached across Petra for a paper towel.

"Did Dr. B keep his files on the floor or something? Dr. Marino looked disheveled. I've been working with him for two years, and he never looks disheveled." Her narrowed eyes met Lacey's in the mirror.

Lacey should tell Petra she and Nick had kinky sex on every piece of furniture in the office. *She wished.* "Ah, Dr. B didn't use a computer and had a very messy office, so Nick, Dr. Marino, went through some of his files."

Petra grabbed the edge of the vanity. "We heard he was with you last night when you got that call from Jill."

"Business." As in Petra should mind hers.

"That's good."

"Is it?" Lacey dropped her paper towels in the trash.

"I warned you before. He's a player. He's going to that benefit tonight at the Bay Plaza Hotel for the San Francisco Children's Burn Unit, and he always brings a date to those benefits. I take it you're not his date?"

"What does he have to do with the Children's Burn Unit?"

"He donates his services there for free." Petra straightened her shoulders as if she did the work. "He also works with kids from war-torn areas to restore faces injured by shrapnel."

Nick's image shifted again. Who knew the hunky doctor worked for free…for kids? The man had more sides than an uncut diamond, but that led to confusion. She wanted a straightforward man. One who didn't lie. One who didn't cheat on his spouse. One who took a steady course.

"You're not his date, are you?" Petra waited, her lips slightly parted, her brows arching over her eyes.

"Nope." Crossing her arms, Lacey faced Petra, who stood between her and the door.

"Dr. Nick Marino's not the only man in town, anyway." Petra leaned toward the mirror and touched up her lipstick. "I happen to have a hot date tonight, too."

"Congratulations." Lacey shoved out of the bathroom and waited for Nick in front of the elevators. Sounded like Petra had a case of unrequited lust for her boss.

"Ready?" Nick joined her at the elevator and punched the

button. When the doors closed on them, he turned to her. "Thanks for everything, Lacey. I appreciate your silence."

She shrugged. It was the least she could do for the heroic doctor who saved her life and ran around donating his considerable talents to help burned children. What were a few skeletons in the closet? Funny, he never mentioned his humanitarian exploits to her. It was almost as if he wanted her to dismiss him as a superficial cosmetic surgeon, hobnobbing with the rich and famous.

She said, "Maybe Dr. B, Debbie and Jill weren't doing the right thing, but I still want to see their murderer pay."

"He will. I'll have my brother tell the FBI about Dr. Buonfoglio after the trial, and they'll track their murders back to the De Lucas."

When the elevator doors opened on her parking level, Nick placed his hand against the small of her back as they walked toward her car. They could be any couple leaving work.

"Then I'll see you tonight?" She ducked her head in the car to drop her purse on the seat.

Clasping her hand, he pulled her around. His lips sealed over hers, his tongue edging into her mouth.

Should she rebut his advances? Laugh at the incongruity of their pairing? *Oh, hell. Just this once.*

She leaned into him, and his arm snaked around her body, pressing her against him. Her breasts, covered in thin cotton, tingled as they met his hard chest. She tilted her hips forward so their bodies made contact along every line, and then she trailed her hand up the side of his thigh, caressing the hard, lean muscle through the wool-silk fabric of his slacks.

He nibbled her bottom lip and skimmed his tongue along her jawline. Then he planted a kiss at the base of her throat.

Lifting his flushed face, he said, "Just in case someone's watching."

He stepped back, and she felt the loss of his closeness so acutely she grabbed the car door to steady herself. She didn't trust her voice to say a word, so she dipped into her car and slammed the door.

Placing his hand over hers, he said, "I'll drop by after the fund-raiser tonight. Remember, stay put."

He watched her drive out of the parking structure and raised his hand in a wave.

Oh, boy, what was she getting herself into? She liked order in her life. Demanded it.

The men she dated had regular, uncomplicated, nine-to-five jobs—engineers, programmers, architects, even the occasional attorney if he didn't practice trial law. They picked her up for dates on time, did dinners and movies, and followed her unspoken rules of dating—one, short kiss on the first date, a longer kiss on the second date, a little mutual groping on the third date, and absolutely no sex until he showed her evidence that he'd been tested for all sexually transmitted diseases.

She sighed and rubbed her eyes. It had been a while since she'd groped someone. She slammed on her brakes at a red light.

Yeah, like two minutes ago.

Had she really rubbed Nick's thigh? Pressed against his crotch? Temporary insanity brought on by secret keys, stress and a mob killer stalking her.

On the way to the hotel, she checked her rearview mirror and made a few detours if someone followed her for too long. She'd learned from the best—Dr. Nick Marino, cosmetic surgeon, humanitarian and part-time hood.

Fifteen minutes later, she wheeled in front of the Grand Marquis, left the engine running and slid the assortment of papers and files from Dr. B's office from the passenger seat into her hand.

The valet opened the car door. "Good evening."

"Damn."

"Excuse me?" The parking attendant stepped back, blinking his eyes.

Holding up her hand, Lacey bent forward and looked under the seat for the appointment pages and Dr. B's personal calendar. She craned her neck to check the backseat. She'd left them, together, on her desk. If Dr. B's daughter dropped in tomorrow, she'd take that calendar.

"Sorry, I forgot something at the office." She snatched the car door from the startled valet and pulled away from the curb.

The appointment book got her in trouble the last time. If she hadn't pulled it out and left her desk unlocked the night Dr. B was murdered, the killer never would've attacked her. Of course, Nick never would've had the opportunity to save her, either. Yep, trouble all around.

As darkness crept over the city and lights twinkled on bit by bit in the office buildings, Lacey raced back to the medical center, keeping an eye on her rearview mirror. Her tires squealed in the parking structure and she swung into a reserved space next to the elevator. The doctor who parked here wouldn't mind her borrowing it for ten minutes.

She punched the elevator button over and over, and when the doors opened on her floor several people got off. Most of the doctors in the building stopped taking appointments well before five o'clock, and once the late-afternoon appointments ended, nurses and office workers poured out of the building.

Lacey entered the elevator alone, and it didn't make one stop on her way up to her floor. When she rounded the corner, Nick's office manager was locking up.

She nodded at Lacey when she passed her in the hallway. Lacey unlocked Dr. B's office and slipped inside, locking the door behind her.

The scent of Nick's spicy cologne still hung in the air,

totally masculine, totally heady, eliciting memories of his lips pressed against hers, his tongue invading her mouth.

Get a grip, woman. Shaking her head, she swept through the swinging doors and spotted the calendar and the loose papers in her in-box. When did she get so forgetful? She bound them with a rubber band and tucked them into her bag as her gaze scanned the rest of her little work space.

Satisfied she hadn't left anything else behind, she exited the office and locked the door. She glanced up and down the empty corridor, empty except for one man slipping into the men's room. She wished she had someone to come down to the parking structure with her. She wished she had Nick. He made a great bodyguard—big gun, hard body, great kisser.

When the elevator doors opened, she peered inside the car before stepping over the threshold. She pushed the button for the first floor of the parking structure, and the elevator ground into motion. As the elevator skimmed past the lobby level, she bit her lip. Usually lots of people got on at that level. At least her car was right next to the elevator.

The orange light lit up behind P1. Lacey grabbed the strap of her bag and inched forward, ready to get off.

The doors didn't open, and the elevator didn't stop. It continued its downward descent, past P2, P3, and P4, finally settling at the basement level.

Swallowing hard, Lacey punched at the other buttons to get the elevator moving before the doors opened.

It didn't work.

The doors squeaked open, and she flattened her body against the side of the car. Once again, she pressed the other buttons—the lobby, P3, floor five, six, eight.

Still the doors gaped open, and the dank smell of the basement oozed into the elevator.

Her breath, short and shallow, hissed out of her nose. The

pounding of her heart echoed in her ears. With trembling fingers, she continued to punch all the buttons.

Then a huge man with a black ski mask filled the elevator doorway.

Chapter Seven

Nick straightened his black bow tie in front of the mirror, his brow furrowed. Lacey's role in this catastrophe he called a life was over. At least he hoped so. As long as she stayed safely at the hotel for the next week and a half, she should be okay.

He sucked in his cheek. He should've told her, just in case, if anyone threatened her she should give up his name and the information about the key. He'd handle it from there, and it might save her life.

The lines in his face deepened. He knew better than that. Even if she didn't cough up the goods on his brother, she'd be dead. The De Lucas didn't operate any other way.

What the hell was he doing, heading off to a benefit, no matter how worthy, while Lacey remained in danger? She had no one to protect her. Even if he didn't show up tonight and perform his dog-and-pony show, the well-heeled guests had already ponied up the money for the Burn Unit. The kids wouldn't suffer if he didn't put in an appearance.

A car engine rumbled outside, and he twitched the curtain aside. A black town car idled at the curb. Nick called upstairs, "The car's here. I'll be back later."

His aunt's off-key singing drowned out his words, and he smiled as he stepped into the clear night. He could tolerate his aunt Paula's idiosyncrasies. She had rescued him twice, once as a child and again as an adult.

As he settled in the back of the limo, he told the driver, "Change of plans. I'm heading to the Grand Marquis."

Did he have a chance with Lacey when this mess ended? Probably not. He tucked the index cards for his speech in the side pocket of the door and rested his head against the seat. For him the mess never ended. His past dogged him no matter how hard he tried to shake it loose. Lacey didn't even know the half of it. And when she did? She'd run in the opposite direction…as she should.

The driver pulled up in front of the hotel, and Nick jumped out, telling him to wait. Maybe he could take Lacey out for a nice dinner as long as he was all dressed up and had a car for the evening.

His gut constricted when his insistent banging on her hotel room door didn't elicit a response. He jogged down the stairs to the front desk, relieved to find a clerk he knew from one of the many benefits and fund-raisers his foundation held at the hotel.

"Jason, right? I'm looking for my…sister, Cindy Marino. She's not in her room."

"Hello, Dr. Marino. Have you tried one of the restaurants or maybe the fitness center?"

Nick blew out a breath. She could be anywhere in the hotel. Just because she wasn't in her room didn't mean she was out on the streets.

"Thanks, I'll check." He turned from the desk, when a valet parking attendant leaned against the counter, clutching a handful of tickets.

"Are you looking for your sister, drives a red Jetta?"

"Have you seen her?" Nick's heart thumped against his chest as he held his breath.

"Yeah, she wheeled up a while ago and then peeled out of here. Said she forgot something at the office."

The blood roared in Nick's ears as he spun around and charged through the revolving doors. Was she out of her mind? She knew the police didn't have the manpower to offer protection. Why would she take a chance with her life? A killer was out there looking for information and wouldn't hesitate to kill anyone who didn't give it to him.

And Lacey was his next target.

LACEY TRIED TO SCREAM, but her throat tightened with the effort. She flung out her hands, hitting a chest that felt like a brick wall. She shoved and punched and kicked his shin, but he reached forward and grabbed her throat, pushing her against the elevator wall.

She clawed at his hands, covered with black gloves, and tried to pry them loose from her neck. He dragged her out of the elevator and shoved her onto the cold cement floor of the basement. Releasing her throat, he pinned her down with a knee planted on the small of her back. She choked and coughed, sucking air into her burning lungs.

"Where are the doc's files on the punks he done faces for?" he growled in her ear.

"I don't know what you're talking about." She lifted her head from the floor, twisting it to the side, the smell of grease and oil filling her nostrils.

"Just gimme the goods, and I'll let you off easy." He ground his knee into her back and she gasped.

"I was just the receptionist. I don't know anything." Maybe if she lied, made up a location for the files and sent him off on a wild-goose chase, he'd leave her alone.

He grunted. "Why are you broads so hot to protect Pretty Boy Paglietti?"

Lacey gulped. She really didn't know what he was talking about. Who the hell was Pretty Boy Paglietti? Maybe this didn't have anything to do with Nick's brother, T.J. Marino, after all.

"I don't know who that is. I'm not protecting anyone." Except Nick. She shifted away from the weight pressing her down and planted her palms on the cement. Could she throw him off?

The man fumbled in his pocket, and Lacey jerked beneath him as the smell of ether filled the air.

"Don't worry, sweetheart. I'm not gonna kill you, but you're coming with me."

The other elevator doors creaked open, and a babble of voices floated into the basement.

Lacey's attacker jerked to the side, his knee slipping off her back. Yelling, she rolled the other way.

"Help! Somebody help me!"

As if conjured from her dreams, Nick charged out of the elevator in a tux. One man stumbled out behind him, and two women screamed. The masked man sprinted for the stairs where the metal door was propped open. He staggered into the stairwell, slamming the door behind him.

Nick gave chase and grappled with the door handle, but the door wouldn't budge. The man from the elevator and one of the women crouched beside Lacey, while the other woman leaned against the wall covering her mouth.

"Are you all right? What happened down here?" The tall man held her wrist lightly to check her pulse. His bedside manner had "doctor" written all over it.

Nick kicked the door and cursed. Then he strode back to Lacey and helped her to her feet, enfolding her in his strong arms.

Lacey collapsed against his chest. How did he know she was in danger? "That man attacked me. I was trying to get to the first floor of the parking garage, but the elevator came down to the basement instead. He was waiting for me."

The woman gasped. "How did you know, Dr. Marino?" She turned to Lacey. "Dr. Marino charged into the elevator with us, and then forced us all to the basement. I thought he'd gone nuts, but now I'm glad we got here in time."

"I saw the other elevator stuck on the basement level. I knew Lacey was here…and just had a feeling." He rubbed circles on her back, and she clung to him tighter.

He'd saved her life twice.

The doctor who checked her pulse looked up. "Didn't you work for Dr. Buonfoglio?"

As Lacey nodded, the woman stepped back from her as if she had a communicable disease.

"His two surgical nurses were murdered, too." The woman crossed her arms, gripping her elbows.

The other woman called from the elevator where she held the door open. "Hey, this thing's working now. Let's get the hell out of here."

The doctor clicked his tongue. "We have to call the police."

Lacey sighed and followed everyone back onto the elevator. She had to keep the attacker's true motive from the police. *Great, time for more lies.*

LACEY TWITCHED BENEATH the arm Nick draped across her shoulders as they walked away from the police and their questions. They waited for the elevator, and Nick mumbled into Lacey's hair that smelled oddly of roses and axle grease, "Just hold on for another minute."

When the elevator doors closed behind them, Lacey sagged against his body, and he tightened his arms around her. He should've never left her.

She raised her head when the elevator doors opened onto the lobby and he steered her out of the building and onto the sidewalk.

"My car's in the parking structure."

"Don't worry about it. We'll go back to the hotel in style." He waved the limo over and the driver jumped out of the car.

Nick said, "We're going to the Grand Marquis."

The driver nodded, and as he swung the back door open, his gaze flickered over Lacey. When Nick bundled her in the car, the driver leaned in and murmured, "There's whiskey in the car, sir."

Nick nodded. This guy deserved a good tip.

Settling beside Lacey on the black leather seat, Nick said, "Now, tell me what really happened."

Lacey drew in a shaky breath, gripping her hands in her lap. Nick's large hand covered both of hers, his warmth seeping into her skin. What happened to his benefit…and his date?

If he were her date, she'd never let him out of her sight dressed in that black tux, all careless elegance and masculine charm.

When he barreled out of the elevator and took off after her attacker, she'd nearly fainted with relief. In a few short days, she'd come to rely on him. She thought her father, the last man she'd depended on, pretty much cured her of harboring any expectations from men. But she could trust this man with her life.

"Are you ready to tell me what happened back there?" He squeezed her hands and reached for a whiskey decanter and a glass from the minibar secured against the back of the front seat.

She hated admitting her carelessness and stupidity. She'd been in such a hurry to get back to the office and grab that calendar she hadn't paid any attention to her surroundings once she got to the office. Was her assailant the man who'd slipped into the men's room right before she got onto the elevator? He must've been waiting for her, hanging around the office.

She knew he hadn't followed her from the hotel. She'd made sure of that. He didn't even know she was at the hotel. He hadn't made one move while she'd been ensconced at the Marquis.

The muted light from the car interior played across the amber liquid in the glass Nick held out to her. She squared her shoulders and looked into his eyes.

"I went back for the calendar you found in Dr. B's office."

His body jerked and the whiskey sloshed over the side of the glass. "You should've waited. Did he follow you?"

"I don't think so. I was very careful driving back to the office, but he may have already been in the building."

She sipped the whiskey, the liquid fire trailing down her throat. She welcomed the burn. "He rigged the elevator to go down to the basement without stopping at the other floors. If you hadn't been there and noticed…"

She shuddered, and Nick scooped his arm around her waist and held her close. Leaning her head against his upper arm, she sighed. Why couldn't this be happening without all the terrifying stuff that came before?

"Why were you there?" She twisted her head to study his profile. "What happened to your benefit?"

"I never made it. I decided to have a nice, quiet dinner with you instead, and then discovered you'd gone back to the office."

"And your date?"

His brows shot up. "Date? I never bring a date to those functions. It's all about raising money."

"For the Children's Burn Unit."

"Who told you about that?" His muscles tensed. Why was he so anxious to hide his good deeds?

"Your biggest fan, Petra."

"That woman has a big mouth."

"She's obviously proud of the work you do, and I ruined the occasion."

He kissed the top of her head. "You didn't ruin anything. I had misgivings about going and knew I wouldn't be able to concentrate on my speech. So I canceled. We raised most of the money already anyway by selling tickets to the event, and the rest will come from the silent auction."

"Good, it's such a worthy cause."

He twirled a lock of her hair around his finger. "Did you tell him anything?"

"A-about you or the key? Of course not." She sat forward. Suddenly his arm didn't feel so comfortable anymore. "Do you think I'd fold that easily?"

"Easily?" He nudged her around to face him, his eyes widening in the dark car. "Lacey, the man was choking you. He could've killed you."

He pulled her back into his arms and wrapped her up so tightly, her breath hitched in her chest. While she savored this new experience of leaning on someone, they had business to discuss.

"I don't think he wanted to kill me." She disentangled herself from the warm comfort of Nick's embrace. "He wanted information and I sensed he'd go to any lengths to get it, but he didn't go in for the kill."

Nick rubbed his chin. "It took him three murders to realize he'd better leave someone from that office alive to get what he wants—my brother's identity. What about the police?"

The cops had questioned them separately. Did Nick think she gave anything up? "They unnerved me almost as much as the attack."

She grabbed the glass of whiskey she'd placed in the cup holder and swirled it around. "Lying to the police is harder than it looks on TV."

"I'm sorry you're so far into this, Lacey." He ran a fingertip along her jaw. "Do you think they suspected anything?"

"Nope." She took another swig of alcohol and her eyes watered as it scorched her throat. Almost as hot as Nick's touch. A warm flame fanned across her chest and loosened the vice clamping the back of her neck. She took another gulp.

Nick lifted one eyebrow and plucked the glass from her hand. "Slow down. That's supposed to take the edge off, not turn you into a blob of jelly."

"Okay, I think it took a few edges off." Feeling dizzy, she leaned her head back and closed her eyes.

"Are you sure he didn't follow you from the Grand Marquis?"

Nick's questioning rivaled the cops'. So much for losing the sharp edges. "I may have made a big mistake going back to the office, but I watched my rearview mirror the entire time and took a few random turns. No way anyone followed me."

He brushed a strand of hair from her face. "I should've followed you to the hotel from the office. I'm responsible for protecting you."

"You're not responsible for me, Nick."

"Yes I am."

He enunciated his words so sharply and with such force, her lids flew open. His dark eyes glittered, and a muscle twitched in his jaw.

"I'll be okay." She ran her fingertips along the hard line of his jaw. "I'm through taking stupid risks. I'll be careful for two weeks, and then this will all be over, right?"

"You don't understand, Lacey." He plowed his fingers through his hair. "I have to protect…everyone."

"I know your brother saved your life, but he's a big boy. He got in trouble, turned snitch, went on the run and changed his face. I'm sure he can take care of himself." She grabbed the half-filled glass from the cup holder, and then put it back when her stomach rumbled in protest.

He said, "Speaking of which, have you eaten anything tonight?"

He just stole *her* line. She shook her head as the limo pulled up to the Grand Marquis.

"Then first things first." Nick ducked out of the car, and then helped her out. He handed the driver a wad of bills and ushered her inside the hotel.

As he propelled her toward the elevators that went to the restaurant at the top of the hotel, she dug her sneakers into the carpet. "Whoa. I'm not going in there looking like this, especially with you looking like that."

He pulled his necktie off, stuffed it in his pocket and unfastened the top two buttons of his crisp white shirt. "Is that better?"

Not exactly. In addition to increasing his sexy quotient a few notches, he still looked formal and she looked—she glanced down at her ripped jeans with the oil smudges—definitely informal.

"You may find it hard to believe, but I do have standards."

"Room service it is." He made a sharp right turn, heading toward the other bank of elevators, dragging her behind him as if he feared she'd make a run for it.

When they got to the room, she slipped her card in the slot and pushed open the door. How far did Nick intend to take his bodyguard role? He couldn't stay with her day and night, could he?

He followed her into the room and picked up a room service menu. "Soup, sandwiches, something more substantial?"

"Soup's fine." She toed off her shoes and slumped onto the love seat while Nick picked up the phone and ordered two bowls of soup, two sandwiches and a pitcher of iced tea. Looked like he planned to stick around.

"Why don't you take a warm shower? You'll feel better."

"You're right. I'm sick of smelling like a garage." She pushed off the love seat, gathered her robe and headed for the cavernous bathroom.

The hot water pounded her back as she rolled her shoulders forward. She soaped up a washcloth and scrubbed the last bits of grit and fear from her body.

Just her luck, she'd snagged a limo ride with Dr. Nick Marino and she looked and smelled like a mechanic. Not too shabby considering Nick was accustomed to dating socialites and supermodels.

Of course, this wasn't a date.

Out of guilt, Nick felt protective toward her. He even admitted it. She cranked off the water and dried herself with a fluffy hotel towel. She dabbed on a little perfume to completely expunge eau de grease. The gesture had nothing at all to do with the presence of Dr. Perfect lounging in her hotel room.

Just to prove it, she shrugged into her oversize terry cloth bathrobe, which didn't have one seductive thread in its entire construction.

She combed out her wet hair and resisted an urge to put on makeup. Satisfied that she had the look of a woman who expected absolutely nothing from her tuxedoed guest, she swept out of the bathroom in a gust of scented steam.

The room service tray had already arrived, and Nick had set it up on the coffee table in front of the love seat. Wisps of steam curled from the bowls, and Lacey inhaled the comforting aroma of chicken noodle soup. Hardly the smell of seduction.

Then she caught an eyeful of Nick.

He'd removed his shoes and socks, slipped out of his jacket and cummerbund, and had pulled his shirt out of his slacks. He'd rolled up his sleeves, displaying the corded muscles of his sinewy forearms. How could a man look yummier halfway out of his tux than all trussed up?

"I hope you don't mind that I made myself comfortable. I felt like I was wearing a straitjacket."

"You're paying for the joint." She shrugged and the V at

the neck of her robe gaped open. Grabbing the lapels, she tugged it closed.

"Sit down and have something to eat." He patted the cushion beside him. "I got the iced tea because I thought it would feel better on your throat than the hot soup."

"I'll let you know." She sank down next to him and held a spoonful of soup to her lips, puckering up to blow on it.

He shifted next to her, cleared his throat and poured two glasses of iced tea. "What do you think, something cold or something hot?"

She glanced sideways, her gaze dropping to his shirt open at the chest to reveal a sprinkling of dark hair. Slurping in the soup, she burned her tongue. Definitely something hot.

"Maybe I need that iced tea, after all." She took the glass from him and stuck her tongue in the cool tea. His brows shot up. "Burned my tongue," she explained.

He gulped his own tea and dug into a sandwich as if he hadn't eaten for days.

"Not quite the fare you would've enjoyed at that fancy shindig."

"I didn't miss a thing by not going except the chance to rescue you, and that's worth all the puffed crab and foie gras in the world."

He put her above puffed crab? Her father had never put his family above one of those fund-raisers. He never missed an opportunity to rub elbows with the San Francisco glitterati, and toward the end, he'd stopped taking his wife. Mom cramped his style.

"I hope your absence didn't put a dent in the money raised for the Children's Burn Unit."

"Those people have money to spare, and they're always looking for a good tax deduction."

"You don't do too badly yourself." She waved her arms around the expensive suite.

He caught one of her waving hands. "Does my money bother you for some reason, Lacey?"

She swallowed at the warm pressure of his fingers. Why couldn't she be immune to his considerable charms? Why did she have to fall at his feet like all the others?

"I'm just not attracted to…a flashy lifestyle. That's what my father was all about, and in the end my mom just wasn't good enough for him, even though she helped put him through medical school."

"That's a common story." He lifted a shoulder but still refused to give up possession of her hand. "I have my own reasons for the lifestyle I choose, but none of them involve using someone else."

"It's not for me to judge you. How you live your life is none of my business." She flicked some crumbs off the fingers of her free hand onto a plate.

He grabbed that hand, too.

"Like it or not, it is now. We're in this together. You have to trust me. Do you?"

He'd pulled her around so she was facing him, her lips inches from his. Despite the intrigue and mystery that hung around him like a dark cape, she did trust him. At least she trusted him to protect her from physical danger. Beyond that…?

She parted her lips, and he weaved his fingers in her hair and pulled her closer. His mouth tasted sweet and cool from the sugared iced tea as he closed it around hers. She wrapped her arms around him, placing her palms against the hard muscles of his back, which shifted as he clasped her to his body.

The kiss deepened, and she gave herself up to the languid sensation creeping through her veins like thick honey. His fingers trickled down her throat and circled the indentation at the base of her neck.

Her terry cloth bathrobe suddenly felt as impenetrable as the armor she wore with most men, and she loosened the belt around her waist. The robe gaped open, and her breasts chafed against Nick's starched shirt.

He laced his fingers through hers and pulled her palm against his lips. After he kissed the center of her palm, he said, "Are you sure this is what you want?"

She caressed his face, still smooth from a recent shave. "Are you sure this isn't for show?"

"Since there are just the two of us, I'm sure." Grinning, he pulled her up from the love seat and took possession of her lips once again.

She stood on her tiptoes and braced her hands against his wide shoulders. The tie of her robe slipped, exposing her nakedness to his hungry gaze. As his eyes trailed the length of her body, all her senses hummed, drowning out the warning bells clanging in her head.

His hands skimmed her curves, and her rules, regulations and medical reports melted in the heat that followed the path of his touch.

"You're so beautiful. Natural. Fresh."

A crease formed between his brows, and a shadow passed across his face. His touch faltered, a look of yearning warring with the dark passion in his eyes.

Did he want to put her on a pedestal like some kind of Florence Nightingale? She'd have to work fast to correct that impression. She yanked at the buttons on his shirt, popping off a few in the process. Would Florence do that?

Apparently not. Nick shrugged out of his shirt and pulled his T-shirt over his head. Black hair scattered along the hard muscles defined his chest. He looked dangerous half naked, all signs of the urbane, sophisticated doctor tousled and teased into this he-man with hard muscles and a body more suited to the docks than the operating room.

Was she ready to unleash the other half?

He ran his hands beneath her robe and peeled it from her shoulders. It dropped in a heavy heap at their feet. Her heart thudded as Nick cupped her breasts, running his thumbs across her peaked nipples.

Hooking her arms around his waist, she swung her hips forward, making contact with the smooth material of his slacks. A low groan rumbled in his throat as he clutched her bottom, pulling her closer so she could feel his hard desire and smell the pure masculine scent pulsing from his pores.

Arching her backward, he scattered kisses along her neck and shoulders. Her knees weakened, and she sagged against him. With his hands still planted on her bottom, he hoisted up her body while she wrapped her legs around his hips.

"Are you sure, Lacey? You don't know me…you don't know who I am."

He'd saved her life. He wanted to protect her. She didn't need to know anything more than that right now.

"Just pretend someone's watching us, and we have to prove we're lovers instead of co-conspirators and obstructers of justice."

That did the trick. In four long strides he crossed the room with her clinging to him and pushed open the bedroom door. He dropped her on the bed, and she scrambled to her knees, plucking at his belt buckle. He combed his fingers through her hair as she unfastened his slacks.

In one deft movement, he pulled down his slacks along with his boxers. She trailed her fingernails up the insides of his thighs and along his straining erection. The man definitely had perfect parts. The muscles in his belly tightened as air hissed between his clenched teeth. She had him just where she wanted him.

Then he grabbed her waist and flung her back on the bed. Straddling her thighs with his knees, he clasped her wrists with one strong hand and pulled her arms over her head, pinning them against the pillow.

Oh, no. Her game plan didn't include this loss of control. With the few boyfriends she'd had, she set the pace. She satisfied their needs, and they were grateful. She never demanded too much from them. *Keep your expectations low and nobody gets hurt when they decide to move on.*

She struggled against Nick's restraining hold, and then shivered as he laid a foundation of kisses from her throat to her belly. He wedged his free hand between her tightly clamped thighs and nudged them apart. The smooth pad of his thumb brushed her throbbing outer folds, and she whimpered.

Her need for a man had never been greater. It frightened her, filled her with dread. "Nick, I…"

"Do you want me to stop?" He released her wrists, but his thumb continued its exploration, delving into her moist layers, circling and caressing until she thrashed her head back and forth against the pillow.

The sweet invasion stopped, and the tingling that had begun in her toes now gathered in her core, awaiting a delicious release. She jerked her head up.

"Should I continue?" The corner of Nick's mouth lifted as he hovered over her.

For an answer, she moaned and lifted her hips from the bed in wanton invitation. He took the invitation but changed the instrument of her exquisite torture.

His mouth replaced his thumb, and it didn't move any faster. In fact, he started over, nibbling gently at her outer lips, kissing her, suckling her, teasing her.

He had her at his mercy. She'd never had less command over a situation in her life. He played her, controlling her every response. She cried out, wrapped a leg around his shoulder, clawed at his hair, but nothing she did changed his pace. He called the shots, and her body obeyed his orders.

She held her breath as he drew his tongue along the length of her. When he flicked it over her most sensitive point, she exploded. Heat rushed through her body, melting her bones. Her hips rose and fell over and over until Nick cupped her bottom and drove into her.

She dug her nails into his back, convulsing around his hardness. She wanted to please him now, but she knew her pleasure was his, or his was hers…she didn't know anymore. Everything mingled. They were one, joined together by their secret and their desire.

As he reached his climax, his thrusts deepened until he reached her very core. He lowered his head and sealed his mouth over hers, pressing the length of his body along hers, slick with sweat, hers, his. She tasted her feminine essence on his lips, and inhaled his primal masculine scent. They connected in every way, body and soul.

And it scared the hell out of her.

Chapter Eight

Nick rolled onto his back, wedging his shoulder against Lacey's. Although he was no longer inside her, he still wanted to maintain their physical connection. Making love to her exceeded his wildest expectations. He thoroughly enjoyed stripping away her sense of control, layer by silky layer, until he had her quivering beneath his touch.

Did she think sex with him would allow her another outlet for taking charge? Another way to satisfy her deep need to take care of everyone else while she remained aloof from the emotional heat? He had his needs, too, and he needed to pull her into the flames with him.

Her chest rose and fell as her breathing steadied. Resting his chin on her shoulder, he traced a finger around her breast, circling her nipple until it pebbled. A long sigh escaped from her parted lips, and she squirmed on the bed. Time to take her for another ride.

He leaned forward, his tongue following the path of his fingertip. His lips closed around the pink pearl, and Lacey entangled her fingers in his hair, raking it back from his forehead.

"Did you break your nose? I never noticed that bend in it before."

"When I was a kid." Her method of distraction wouldn't work with him.

She ran her finger across the bridge of his nose. "Given your profession, it's funny you never straightened it."

"I never wanted to fix it." He shaped her breast with his hand and nibbled on her earlobe.

"It does save you from looking too much like a pretty boy." Her fingers drummed against his chest, and then she sat up, banging her head against the headboard.

"What's wrong?"

"Who's Pretty Boy Paglietti?"

Nick's stomach sank, and he gave her ear one last nip... because it would be the last one for a while.

"I forgot that part." She sawed her thoroughly kissed bottom lip with her teeth. "The man who attacked me accused me of protecting Pretty Boy Paglietti. Are you sure these guys are after your brother and not this Pretty Boy Paglietti?"

Nick scratched his jaw and bunched the pillows beneath him, sitting up next to her.

"Lacey, my brother *is* Pretty Boy Paglietti."

Her brows snapped over her straight nose—no mangled cartilage there—as she pressed back against the headboard. He knew he had some explaining to do, but he was tired of talking already. He tried to pull back before things went too far, but once he had her satiny body beneath his hands, he couldn't stop.

Now he wanted to continue exploring every inch of her creamy skin, starting with her thigh. He ran his index finger along her leg as it curved to her hip, but she slapped his hand away before he got any farther.

"Who are you?"

"Nick Marino." Sighing, he rubbed his eyes so he didn't have to look at the questions and accusations in hers. Could he do this? Could he tell someone the truth about his identity after more than twenty years of keeping it a secret?

"Are you Nick Paglietti or did your brother change his name from Marino?" She drummed her heels on the mattress. "Who the hell are you?"

"I was born Dominick Paglietti, younger brother of T.J. 'Pretty Boy' Paglietti, currently on the run from the feds and the mob, and son of Antonio Paglietti, full-time scammer, part-time thief and currently plying his trades somewhere south of the border." He watched her face for signs of disgust or, worse, signs of lurid fascination.

A warm light glowed in her green eyes, like a sunset behind stained glass, but her rigid posture screamed "hands off." She pulled the sheet up to chin level and squeezed her arms at her sides. "Do you mind telling me the rest of the story, since I just had sex with a stranger?"

"I *am* Nick Marino. Dominick Paglietti died over twenty years ago." His hands fisted into the bedspread as a wave of pain hit him full force. Did he think making love to a beautiful, clear-eyed woman would make that go away?

"Twenty years ago? You were just a boy." Lacey rubbed the grooves between his knuckles. "Tell me what happened… you owe me."

She was right. She'd agreed to keep quiet about the real motive behind Dr. Buonfoglio's murder, and that deserved an explanation…up to a point.

"I grew up in a rough neighborhood in Newark. My father always nibbled at the fringes of the criminal element. For the most part he ran scams on hapless victims, but one time he crossed the wrong person."

"What happened?"

"He scammed a scammer, a tough guy with mob connections."

Lacey snatched her hand back and covered her mouth, eyes widening. "The De Luca family."

Nodding, he peeled her hand from her mouth and pressed it against his chest, covering it with his own hand.

"My father was out of town when the De Lucas dropped by to get their money back." His lips twisted. "Dad had a sixth sense when his deals got too hot to handle."

"They came to your home?"

"Such as it was." He shrugged. "A two-room apartment in a run-down building."

Her fingers curled against his chest, her nails digging into his skin. "What did they do?"

"Home invasion. Two men came to the door, my mom answered, and they burst through, waving guns, and tied us up."

"Oh, my God." Her fingernails clawed into his flesh, but he welcomed the pain. It distracted him from the pain of his memories.

"My mom insisted she knew nothing about the money my father got from the scam, but they didn't care. They trashed the place, and while they were rifling through all our stuff my brother worked his hands free. He pushed me out the front door and charged the guy with the gun."

"So that's how your brother saved your life?"

"Yeah, some neighbors were coming down the hall just as I stumbled out the door. The two men didn't want to face a horde of angry residents and took off. T.J. saved me that day, but neither of us could save our mother."

She gasped. "They shot her?"

"My mom had asthma and without her inhaler and with a gag stuffed in her mouth, she had an attack and died."

Choking out a sob, Lacey smoothed her hand across his chest where her nails had left crescents.

He waited for the suffocating anger and sorrow that

shrouded his heart whenever he remembered his mother dying before the paramedics arrived, but all he felt was Lacey's smooth palm as she caressed him.

"Nick, I'm so sorry. Is that when Dominick Paglietti disappeared?"

"When my dad returned, he called my mother's family, the Marinos. My aunt swooped in and took me away, but not T.J. He was seventeen at the time and was already dabbling on the dark side—we both were."

"Is that when he became a criminal?"

"The fact that he remained in that environment didn't help." His chest tightened. T.J. stayed and he got the "get out of jail" card to freedom. "He managed to stay on the other side of the law for a while, but couldn't resist when he got an opportunity to stick it to the De Lucas."

"What happened? How'd he get the chance to put Jimmy De Luca behind bars?"

"The De Luca family put the word out on the street that they were looking for a one-time drug courier to transport drugs and money up from Jamaica. T.J. got into a position to get the job, and then he turned everything he had over to the FBI."

"Wow, you mean T.J. waited all that time to get revenge on the De Lucas? This is like a Martin Scorcese movie."

The corner of his mouth twitched. Lacey wasn't as shocked as he'd expected, but then he didn't know what to expect since he'd never told anyone this story before. "He never knew if he'd ever get the opportunity, but he took it when it came knocking."

She twisted to the side and settled her head against his chest, her hair tickling his bare skin. "After he snitched, the FBI placed him in the Witness Protection Program?"

"Yeah, he was safe for a while, but three crooked agents in bed with the De Luca family turned all the information about his new life over to the De Lucas, and they came after him."

"That's when he changed his face? Were you a cosmetic surgeon by then?"

"Yes, and he contacted me first, but he didn't want me to do the surgery, didn't want to involve me…in that way."

Even though he would've done anything for T.J. T.J. was the one who stuck around and avenged their mother's death and took the heat for it while Nick got a new life.

"I'd heard rumors about Dr. Buonfoglio, so I referred T.J. to him." He stroked Lacey's silky hair. If he'd known then the referral would put this beautiful woman's life in danger, he never would've done it.

"Dr. B changed T.J.'s face, and my brother disappeared again with a new identity, and this time he kept it from the FBI."

"And he's resurfacing now to testify again?"

"Big Jimmy De Luca's high-priced attorney won a retrial for him, and T.J.'s not going to allow him to go free. He also wants to finger the fibbies who dropped a dime on him. T.J.'s attorney arranged everything for him, but the De Lucas want to get to my brother first, and to do that they have to know what he looks like."

"He just has to hang on for one more week, right? Will he be safe once he testifies?"

One week seemed like an eternity to him. He shrugged. "At least he'll have the FBI back on his side, and they can do a lot more to ensure his safety than he can do on his own."

Lacey sat up, clutching the sheet to her chest. "Nick, when's the last time you saw your brother?"

"After my graduation from med school." A dull pain throbbed at the base of his skull, and he squeezed his eyes shut.

"So you don't even know what he looks like now."

"Nope."

Her cool touch fluttered across his brow. She pressed a kiss on his temple and snuggled against him, her fingers trailing down his chest. "Thanks for telling me everything."

A flame kindled in his belly, heating up his desire again. He bent his head and kissed her sweet lips as she ran her fingertips along his thigh. He groaned, and an inferno of passion raged over the small flicker of guilt in his heart.

He hadn't told her everything…not quite.

THE FOLLOWING EVENING, Lacey sat cross-legged on the floor of her hotel sitting room, her back resting against the sofa, the pages from the appointment database and Dr. B's personal calendar stacked neatly next to her laptop on the coffee table.

T.J. "Pretty Boy" Paglietti didn't look a whole lot like his brother. She leaned in closer to study the man in the designer suit, flashing a peace sign to the cameras as he entered the courthouse to testify against Jimmy De Luca at his first trial.

He was an attractive man, or at least attractive enough by criminal standards to be called "pretty boy." Must be the blond hair. While Nick's hair was black as midnight, T.J.'s had a golden sheen. His features were blunter than Nick's, but he had the same lean, muscular body.

She sighed and tipped her head back. How had she wound up in the middle of this mess? Why didn't anyone at Dr. B's office tell her what was going on? At least Debbie and Jill knew enough to make a choice. They took the risk…and paid for it with their lives.

She hugged herself to ward off the chill that stole over her body. She hadn't left the hotel room all day and hadn't seen Nick at all.

He'd called to tell her he was back at work and hadn't noticed anything suspicious on the floor. They left everything else unsaid. She knew he wanted to keep his distance from her just in case the killer was watching. She understood his desire to protect himself, but it felt an awful lot like he was hanging her out to dry.

"Nonsense," she said aloud, to dispel the uneasy sensation in her gut. The killer could link her to Dr. B and his secret patients, but he didn't know Nick was T.J.'s brother. Why clue him in? All the guy knew about Nick was that he was the heroic doctor on her floor who came to her rescue… twice.

Sitting forward, she snapped the laptop shut on the man whose cocky expression suddenly looked all too much like Nick's. Her cell phone rang as she shoved aside her computer and slid the calendar and appointment pages in front of her.

"Hello?"

"Hi, Lacey? It's Sarah Jackson, Dr. B's daughter."

"Hi, Sarah. Are you in town yet?"

"I arrived yesterday. I'm going to pack up Dad's houses and drop by the office. Did you leave a key with Security?"

Lacey traced the embossed letters on Dr. B's calendar. It's a good thing she went back for it. She just hoped she and Nick hadn't left anything else of importance in the office. "The security desk has the key to the office. H-has Detective Chu spoken to you yet?"

"Just on the phone. He wants to meet with me while I'm here, but I don't know anything about why someone would want to kill Dad and his two nurses."

Sarah's voice sounded hollow and truly bewildered. She obviously knew nothing about her father's extracurricular activities, and Lacey didn't have the heart to enlighten her.

"You're safe, aren't you, Lacey? I mean, you've been in the office less than a year. Jill and Debbie worked for Dad for a long time, and I'm assuming this is some old grudge."

"Maybe it is."

"Anyway, after I settle Dad's affairs, I'm going to visit Abby and start the process of bringing her back to New Jersey with me and my husband. Would you like to come along? She always liked you, Lacey, you and your mom, ever since she met the two of you a few years back."

"Sure, I'll come along to say goodbye to Abby. Just give me a call when you're going out there."

Lacey ended the call and tapped her pencil on the stack of papers. Should she make one last sweep of the office before Sarah descended on it? Her gaze slid to the window and the sky edged with purple dusk.

No, he might be waiting for her again.

She flipped through the pages of appointments, noting the ones highlighted in blue. Not all of them represented Dr. B's work for the dark side—he couldn't have done that many jobs for criminals. Some had to be clients who simply wished for secrecy.

She ran her finger across the calendar pages, dispensing of days, weeks and months with a flick of the page. Dr. B hadn't had much of a social life, especially after his wife died. He spent most of his free time reading, visiting Abby in Santa Cruz, or holing up at his beach house in San Luis Obispo.

In fact, he went out to that beach house more than Lacey realized. She circled the notation, SLO, which popped up with regularity a few times every month. It must stand for San Luis Obispo.

She scrambled back through the appointment pages, plucking out the ones with the special surgeries. With her pulse tripping, she compared the dates of the special surgical appointments to the dates Dr. B went to San Luis Obispo.

Almost every time he performed one of the surgeries highlighted in blue, he took a trip out to his beach house the following weekend. Maybe he kept the files there.

How long would it take the De Lucas to discover Dr. Buonfoglio had a second home?

She grabbed her cell phone and speed-dialed Nick's office number. Petra answered. Just her luck.

"Dr. Marino has gone home for the day. Can I take a message?"

Did Petra recognize her voice? She'd better not take any chances or spark suspicion. "This is Lacey Kirk. I'll call him on Monday. It's about one of Dr. Buonfoglio's referrals."

When she got off the call, Lacey speed-dialed Nick's cell phone number. He'd given it and his home address to her before he left the other day. She listened to his voice mail and left a message.

She ordered room service and then played with her pasta while she glanced at the appointment pages. They had to get to Dr. B's beach house before the De Lucas discovered it or even before Sarah got there. What if the De Lucas checked out the house when Sarah was there?

Lacey shivered. The De Lucas mowed down anyone who got in their way.

She scooped up her cell phone again and called Sarah.

"Sarah, it's Lacey Kirk. Do I have time to pick up some office files at your father's house in San Luis Obispo before you make it out there?" She held her breath.

"Sure, or you can wait and meet me there since I'm going to close up the house."

"I'd rather get it done right away, so you can settle his business first."

"That's fine. Do you have a key to the house?"

"No." Lacey couldn't even remember the location of the place.

"Well, I'm sure you wouldn't be able to get that key from the police. You can get one from his neighbors, the Griffiths. They're right next door."

"Sarah, do you have the address? It's been a while since I've been out there."

Lacey's breathing returned to normal as Sarah gave her the address of her father's house in San Luis Obispo. She knew where the house was and how to get inside. Now she just needed the man to come with her.

She tried Nick's cell again, getting his voice mail. He'd made it clear she could call him anytime for any reason, especially since the police had hit an impasse with the case.

She couldn't provide a clear description of her attacker and he'd left no prints, so the police had no way of tracking him. They'd already explained to her they didn't have the resources to assign an officer to be her personal watchdog.

But she had Nick.

She toyed with the piece of paper on which she'd written his home address. He was the one who'd issued the open invitation if she needed him. Well, she needed him.

She grabbed her jacket and snagged a taxi in front of the hotel. After she gave the driver Nick's address, she sank back in the seat and closed her eyes. Although she wasn't exactly in trouble, he'd forgive her for trespassing on his private domain once she told him about the beach house and the notations in the calendar.

Uneasiness gnawed at the edge of her stomach. She hoped he wasn't entertaining.

The taxi pulled up in front of a row of Queen Anne Victorians with their turrets and lacy molding. She'd expected Nick to inhabit one of those cold modern mansions, like the ones her father coveted.

She slid out of the taxi, paid the driver and almost asked him to wait. She had no idea what kind of reception to expect. Clutching the white banister like a lifeline, she trudged up the steps to the house.

While she lifted the heavy brass knocker, a security camera

lodged in the corner of the peaked awning caught her eye. Nick lived his life as if he expected a mob hit any moment.

She banged the knocker a few times and then clutched the evidence to her chest. It represented her entrée into Nick's private world, her excuse for intruding into his space. Did she need one?

The door swung open, and Nick stood on the threshold, dressed casually in jeans and a black T-shirt emblazoned with the name of a rock band. She didn't know what surprised her more, his attire or the look of pleasure that flared across his face.

Before she could utter a word, the look of pleasure changed to one of concern as he drew his dark brows together and yanked her inside the house.

"What happened? Are you okay? I knew I shouldn't have left you at that hotel alone."

As his fingers closed around her wrist, she winced and twisted her hand. "I'm fine."

"I'm sorry." He rubbed the inside of her wrist with the pad of his thumb. "I thought maybe you experienced a repeat performance of the other night. How do you know you weren't followed here?" He gazed over her shoulder with narrowed eyes before slamming the door shut and locking it.

"I had my hood up when I left the hotel, and jumped right into a waiting taxi. There was no one around."

"I thought I told you to stay put." He ran his hands up her arms and rested them on her shoulders. "I'd stay with you if I could…"

Giggles erupted from the top of the staircase, followed by pounding footsteps and a woman's voice. "Miranda, get back here."

Nick jerked to the side, and a little girl hurtled down the stairs and jumped off the last step. She stopped and stared at

Lacey with big brown eyes through a tangle of black curls…as black as midnight.

Oh, my God. Nick had a daughter.

Chapter Nine

Miranda plopped down on the last step and pointed a finger at Lacey. "Who's that?"

"It's rude to point, Miranda." Aunt Paula swept down the staircase, as only she could, her hand floating above the carved banister.

Lacey's gaze shifted between Miranda and him, an angry spark leaping into her eyes, a pink tide ebbing across her cheeks. He should've told her everything the other night after they made love. She'd never trust him again...unless he could explain why he had to keep Miranda a secret.

While he stammered out an explanation, Aunt Paula clicked her tongue, dipping down to snatch Miranda's arm and pull her up. "Excuse their manners, dear. I didn't raise them that way. I'm Paula Marino, Nick's aunt, and this is Miranda."

Aunt Paula extended her delicately boned hand to Lacey, and Lacey dragged her attention away from Miranda long enough to take it. "Nice to meet you. I'm Lacey Kirk."

"I thought so." She nodded her head and tugged Miranda's hand.

Miranda popped her finger out of her mouth and said, "Nice to meet you, Lacey."

Lacey placed the folder she was holding on the side table

in the foyer and dropped to her knees in front of Miranda. She stuck out her hand to take Miranda's, saliva and all. "It's very nice to meet you, too, Miranda. How old are you?"

Miranda giggled and hid behind Aunt Paula's leg while shoving five fingers in Lacey's face. Nick took the opportunity to slice a hand across his throat and jerk his thumb upstairs.

His aunt pursed her lips and shook her head. He knew she thought he'd been overly cautious these past three years, but she didn't understand how the De Lucas worked.

"Miranda's obviously a surprise to you, dear. I'll leave so Nick can start explaining." She hoisted Miranda in her arms. "You need to get into the tub. We'll look for Fifi later."

When Miranda and his aunt disappeared on the second floor, Lacey took two steps back toward the door and gripped the handle. "I tried calling first, but you didn't answer your cell."

"My cell didn't ring."

"Looking for this?" Aunt Paula leaned over the banister at the top of the stairs, waving his cell phone. "Apparently, Miranda's stuffed animals were having a conversation."

He caught the phone as she tossed it down, and flipped it open. "Miranda turned it off."

He shoved the phone into his pocket and lifted his shoulders. She looked ready to flee, and he didn't want to make any sudden moves in her direction to hasten her departure.

"I'll just tell you what I came to tell you and then leave you and your daughter in peace."

His daughter? Is that why Lacey looked so angry when she saw Miranda? He dragged his hands out of his pockets, and gripped her shoulders, giving her a shake.

"Miranda's not my daughter."

Lacey stiffened beneath him, her eyes widening. "B-but, she looks just like you."

"Actually, she looks like her mother, but she's a lot

sweeter." He slipped his hands down her arms and laced his fingers with hers. "Come on in and let me explain."

He led her through the double doors to the living room and his aunt's favorite chair by the fireplace. Lacey perched on its edge, her hands curled around the carved armrests.

He lodged a shoulder against the fireplace mantel and raked a hand through his hair.

"Miranda's my niece, T.J.'s daughter."

Lacey's mouth formed an *O*. "Did you take her when your brother went on the run from the FBI?"

"Exactly." He exhaled. Did she understand? "When the De Lucas struck and T.J. realized the FBI had ratted him out, Miranda was two. He wanted to protect his daughter, so he and his wife, Cee Cee, arranged to have Miranda delivered to me, or rather me and my aunt Paula. This is my place and my aunt has her own place up the coast, but she practically lived here when Miranda was a toddler."

She pushed up from the chair and paced an angry circle on the carpet, avoiding Miranda's dollhouse in the process. Maybe she didn't understand.

Flinging out her arms, she stopped in front of him. "Why didn't you tell me? Do you always have to keep some secret, keep some part of yourself sealed away?"

"I've never told anyone about Miranda. Nobody in my office knows I have her. I don't mention her to colleagues. The staff at the hospital doesn't know."

A deep flush stained Lacey's cheeks, and her jawline hardened. He'd said something wrong.

"You're comparing me to coworkers, colleagues and acquaintances? Don't I deserve more consideration?" Her green eyes grew bright and glassy, her lips twisting. "And I don't mean because of that quickie the other night."

His brows shot up. She considered that a quickie?

"I've gone to the mat for you, Nick, the whole nine yards. I ignored my desire to see justice served for Dr. B and his nurses, and I even ignored my own safety to give your brother a chance to testify, and you repay me by keeping more secrets." She threw herself back into the chair and planted her elbows on her knees.

"Mixed sports metaphors aside, I realize that you've gone against your better judgment in this entire matter, but I'm doing my damnedest to protect you. And the less you know about T.J.—and his daughter—the safer you'll be." He sat on the arm of the chair and rubbed Lacey's stiff back, which got stiffer.

"Don't give me any crap about keeping me in the dark for my own good."

"Not just for your safety, Lacey, but for Miranda's." He kneaded her tight shoulder muscles as her silky hair tickled the backs of his hands. "I know you wouldn't willingly give up information about me and my family. You proved that the other night in the basement of the parking garage. But the De Lucas have ways and means at their disposable that you can't imagine in your worst nightmares."

A tremble rippled down her back, and he pulled her up and into his arms. "Do you understand how important it is to keep Miranda a secret? I know you've been burned before by dishonesty, but I swear you can trust me, Lacey."

She nodded her head, and he stroked her hair until her anger and tension soaked into his body. He could handle it. He could take all the fear she had as his own. He wore stress and uncertainty like a second skin—breathed it, lived it.

"I'm glad you know about Miranda…for selfish reasons. It's another burden lifted." He wedged a finger beneath her chin, tipping it up. "But it scares the hell out of me. Taking that little girl into my home three years ago scared the hell out of me, too."

Lacey smiled and the room lit up like a thousand suns. "I can't imagine suave Dr. Perfect with a toddler on his hands."

He grinned back at her like the village idiot, her snide nickname for him glancing off his back. "It was a disaster at first, but my aunt helped out, along with Jacqueline, her nanny."

"I don't understand how you can keep the fact that you have a child living with you under wraps. What about your friends? Your…girlfriends?"

"I don't have many of the former and none of the latter. I have dates, not girlfriends. It's easier, and my aunt has a house up in Stinson Beach where Miranda spends most of her time. She'll be going to school there when she starts kindergarten in the fall. I might buy a second house up there myself."

"A second house." Lacey twirled out of his arms and tripped out of the room. Was she going to hold a second home against him now?

"I think I know where Dr. B may have hidden those files." She returned from the foyer, waving a manila folder in front of her. She dropped to the sofa and opened the folder, fanning pages across the coffee table. "Dr. B has a second home in San Luis Obispo, and the notations in his personal calendar indicate he went there almost every weekend after he performed one of his top-secret surgeries."

"You're brilliant." Nick cupped her face in his hands and kissed her on the mouth. Then his brow furrowed. "Can you find this house?"

"I have the address right here." She patted her back pocket. "I told Dr. B's daughter I had to pick up some office files from the house, and she gave me the address."

"You're becoming an accomplished liar." He grimaced. "Hang around with me long enough and that's what happens."

She rubbed his forearm. "I don't mind hanging around with you to see this through, Nick. Your brother saved your life, and you saved mine. You owe him, and I owe you."

"You don't owe me at the expense of your own safety. My

brother refused to allow me to do his surgery, and I should've refused to allow you to get further involved."

"Doesn't matter." She smoothed his hair back from his brow. "Whether or not you confided in me about the motive behind the murders, Dr. B already involved me. The killer would still be after me, and I'm safer knowing why and having you watch my back."

"And I'm going to keep it that way." He caught her hand and kissed it. "I'm going to San Luis Obispo tomorrow."

"*We're* going to San Luis Obispo tomorrow."

He opened his mouth to protest, but she covered it with her soft but determined hand. "If I have to hole up in that hotel room one more day, I'll go crazy. Besides, I feel safer when I'm with you."

The muzzle turned into a caress as Lacey ran the pad of her thumb across his lips. A man could stand only so much. He sucked her thumb into his mouth, and then pulled her close, crushing her against his chest. She tangled her fingers in his hair, and he took possession of her mouth, using his tongue the way he wanted to use another part of his anatomy.

She planted her hands on his shoulders, pushing him away. She whispered, "What about Miranda?"

He groaned as his body shuddered to a stop. He wanted to take her right here on the silk brocade sofa his decorator selected with such care, but he had a maiden aunt and a little girl upstairs, a brother to protect and a killer to outwit.

Sex would have to wait.

"I BROUGHT YOU A LATTE." Lacey secured the two coffee cups in the cup holders before settling on the leather seat of Nick's BMW.

She drank in his appearance in faded jeans, white T-shirt, with a flannel shirt buttoned loosely over it, and hiking boots.

The black stubble on his chin and the tousled hair completed the rugged individualist look, so different from his crisp doctor persona. She preferred this version of Nick to the slick one because she knew she'd never have a chance with that other version.

"Thanks, I hope you at least put those on my tab."

"Everything's on your tab." She popped the lid off her coffee and blew on the white foam before taking a sip.

Nick pulled away from the corner two blocks from the hotel where they'd decided to meet, just in case someone was watching for her outside the hotel, and joined the line of traffic. "With Dr. Bradley Kirk as your father, you must be accustomed to money. Didn't your mom get a lot of cash and assets out of your father when they divorced?"

"She got enough to buy that house in Sunset, put me through college and nursing school, put my brother halfway through college before he dropped out, and then a lot of it went for her medical treatment."

"Seems like she had her priorities straight."

"I think my father hid a lot of his assets because he sure bounced back quickly after the divorce. He always had women and cash on the side, which entailed keeping my mom in the dark." Her throat tightened when she remembered her father's deceptions. Was she out of her mind to trust Nick?

He reached into her lap and clasped her hand in a warm grip. "I won't let you down, Lacey."

She curled her fingers around his hand and returned the pressure. "Tell me about the work you do for the Children's Burn Unit."

For the next several minutes he told her about the kids he treated, made whole. She sensed the work helped him cope with the loss of his own childhood, spent on the mean streets of Newark. He continued to talk about his work, his colleagues and Miranda.

The words and stories poured out of him like water through a ruptured dam. She didn't know what prompted his sudden gregariousness—the small enclosed space of the car hurtling down the highway, the relief of being with someone who knew about his past, or the lovemaking they'd shared.

After a few hours of driving, Nick pulled into a service station to fill up the tank. Lacey grabbed her purse from the floor of the car. "Do you want something to eat or drink?"

"Yeah, get me a bottle of water." He reached into his pocket and pulled out a wad of bills.

She waved her hand. "I got this one."

She scanned the shelves of junk food, then grabbed a bag of trail mix and a bag of almonds. Nick probably didn't eat junk, not with that body. She picked out two bottles of water and a diet soda and arranged everything on the counter for the clerk to ring up.

Swinging the plastic bag from her wrist, she exited the store. Nick had pulled the car into a parking space in front, and she dropped the bag on the seat.

"I have to use the restroom."

"They're around the other side."

A Jeep filled with loud rap music and louder teenage boys squealed to a stop in front of her. She jumped back and mumbled, "Jerks."

She rounded the corner and swung open the metal door of the single restroom and locked it with the flimsy bolt. While she was washing her hands, someone jiggled the doorknob.

Tossing her used paper towels into the trash, she checked her reflection in the warped mirror. She could use some lipstick, but she'd wait until she got back to the car.

She slid the bolt back and pushed the door open, almost hitting a burly man wearing khaki trousers and a black polo standing on the outside. Gasping, she jerked to the side.

Steadying the door, he took a step forward, reaching into the pocket of his windbreaker. She swallowed and the hair on the back of her neck quivered.

Two teenagers stumbled around the corner. One of them yelled to the other, "Dude, why are you following me to the bathroom?"

The man's grip tightened on the door as he pulled his hand out of his pocket. He nodded to Lacey. "Sorry, thought my wife was in here."

As Lacey turned away, the two boys pushed and shoved each other until, laughing, one slipped into the men's bathroom, slamming the door behind him.

She hurried to the car, glancing over her shoulder. The man appeared and walked into the convenience store.

Lacey dropped onto the passenger seat, her hands trembling as she fastened her seat belt.

"What's wrong?" Nick twisted the cap on his water bottle and shoved it in the cup holder.

Folding her hands in her lap, she shook her head. "There was a man by the restroom when I came out, a big man. He scared the hell out of me."

"Did he do anything? Say anything?"

Her gaze glued to the automatic doors of the minimart, she answered, "He tried the door handle when I was in there, and then said he was looking for his wife. But that was after two obnoxious teenage boys came along. Before that…"

"What?" Harsh lines creased Nick's face as he gripped the steering wheel.

"I don't know." She hugged herself, pulling her leather jacket closed. "The look in his eyes frightened me."

"You said he was a big guy. Did you recognize his voice? Could it be…?"

"The voice of the man in the garage was gravelly, harsh. This guy's wasn't. How could he be way down here? Nobody followed us from the hotel. We checked enough times. We would've noticed a car following us on the open highway." She clenched her jaw to stop her chattering teeth.

"Just a man looking for his wife." He caressed the side of her face.

"You're right. Let's get out of here, and watch out for that Jeep. Those boys are a little wild."

As they peeled away from the service station, Nick checked his mirror and Lacey craned her neck to peer out the back window. Several cars pulled out behind them and then passed on the left or took the next few exits. Nobody followed them.

Lacey gulped in a deep breath as her thundering heart slowed its pace. She'd probably scared the guy as much as he'd scared her after banging into him with the door. He was probably getting ready to yell at his wife.

She bent forward and rummaged in the bag on the floor. "Trail mix?"

"That's all you have? I should've told you to get me some of those flaming-hot corn chips."

TWO HOURS LATER THEY arrived at Dr. B's beach cottage. Sarah had phoned the neighbors ahead of time so they were expecting Lacey.

"So horrible about Dr. Buonfoglio. Do the police have any suspects?" Mrs. Griffiths, an elderly woman with bright, birdlike eyes, dropped the keys into Lacey's palm.

"No, not yet." Lacey tapped her toe, impatient to start the search. The files had to be here. Then Nick could destroy them and no one would find out what T.J. looked like before he testified.

"You couldn't pay me to move back to the big city. Right, Fred?"

Mr. Griffiths, rocking on a porch swing, cupped his ear. "What's that?"

"I'm glad to be out of the city, aren't you?" She yelled loud enough for the whole block to hear.

"Young and pretty? Hell, Edie, you ain't neither." His chuckle turned into a hacking cough, and Mrs. Griffiths rolled her eyes at Lacey before climbing the porch to pound her husband on the back.

"Thank you." Waving the key, Lacey backed up to the sidewalk and joined Nick at the door of Dr. B's place. She opened the front door and gagged at the dank, musty smell of the house. Seemed Dr. B hadn't been here in a while.

After Nick followed her over the threshold, she locked the screen door, leaving the front door open.

Nick pulled two pairs of latex gloves out of his pocket and handed a pair to her.

Lacey widened her eyes. "You're being overly cautious. Remember, we belong here. We didn't break in this time."

Nick pulled on his gloves as if getting ready for surgery. "Maybe, but if the cops ever search this place, do you want them to find your prints everywhere? Don't forget, I'm almost a pro at this kind of subterfuge."

"You have a point there." She snapped on the gloves, and they repeated their now-familiar search behind photos and art work on the walls, through desk drawers, closets and even under furniture.

Crossing his arms, Nick slouched against a tall bookshelf near the door. "It's another dead end, Lacey."

"Maybe Dr. B never kept any information on those

patients." She peeled off the gloves and shoved them into her front pocket.

"I wish I could believe that." He ran a hand over his face, dislodging a cobweb in the process. "But then why all the sub-terfuge? Why the secret key?"

"It's a waiting game now. De Luca's people are never going to find out what T.J. looks like before that trial. Even with the inside track, we can't find the files, and with three out of the four people in Dr. B's office dead…" Icy fingers settled around the nape of her neck. Three out of four.

"Exactly." Nick lunged off the bookshelf and encircled her waist with his hands. "Maybe you need to leave town alto-gether until the trial is over."

"I can't leave town. Classes resume on Monday."

"You are not going to class." He squeezed her so hard, she almost lost her breath. "Stay away from the hospital and stay away from Dr. Buonfoglio's office. The killer knows he can find you there."

She suppressed a shiver. "Are we giving up the search for the files?"

He lifted a shoulder. "I don't know where else to look, do you? We have eight more days until my brother testifies, and once he's safe you'll be safe, too."

With Nick's arms wrapped around her, she never felt safer. He lied like he performed surgery…with great skill and finesse, but he took her into his confidence. He didn't have to do that.

Yes, he did. Her little voice of self-preservation that she'd allowed Nick to smother with his kisses, echoed in her head. *He needed you. He needed your silence and your cooperation.*

Right after Dr. B's murder, Nick had tagged the killer as a disgruntled patient. In fact, he confided in her only when he had to—when she caught him red-handed at Jill's place and when she walked in on the happy domestic scene with his niece.

Lacey straightened her spine, pulling away from the sweet warmth of Nick's embrace. "I'm hungry. Do we have time to grab lunch before heading back, or do you want to eat on the road?"

"Are you all right?" He stroked her back, a furrow forming between his eyebrows. "I wish I could just flip the pages of the calendar and make time jump ahead one month."

So he could get back to his life of glittering social events with glittering society women? Crawling beneath furniture with her and the dust bunnies must be a big step down for Dr. Nick Marino, probably even for Dominick Paglietti.

"Lunch?" She stepped back.

"We have time for more than lunch." He ate up the space between them, took her hand and made lazy circles with his thumb on the inside of her wrist. "I don't have to return to the city until Sunday night. We can get a room at that Victorian hotel we passed."

Her self-preservation voice grew fainter with every circle on her wrist. The gooey desire swirling in her belly mucked up her brain, too.

He brushed his lips across hers where a pulse throbbed to an insistent rhythm. Her hips swayed to that rhythm as she hooked her arms around his neck. His kiss seared her mouth, unfurling the passion she'd wound into a tight ball in her chest.

"Are you two finished in there?" The bang on the metal screen door split them apart and they jumped back from each other. "Oops, sorry to interrupt, but Fred and I are going out to the senior center for a little bingo. You can leave the key under our mat."

Lacey returned to earth to find Mrs. Griffiths cupping her hands over her face, peering through the screen door, and Mr. Griffiths at her elbow with a big smile revealing a set of ill-fitting dentures.

"We're all done." Lacey skirted Nick and his darkly seductive aura and flipped the lock on the screen door. Dangling the key chain from her fingertip, she stepped onto the porch.

Nick joined her, his breathing still irregular.

"Did you find what you wanted?" Mrs. Griffiths's black eyes darted between Lacey's and Nick's empty hands.

"I think they found what they wanted." Mr. Griffiths winked and nudged Nick in the side with his elbow.

Lacey stifled a smile behind her hand. "Actually, I didn't find the files I wanted. I'll have to search Dr. B's office in the city. We'll lock the dead bolt."

"We'll do it." Mrs. Griffiths snatched the key from Lacey's hand, pursing her lips at her husband.

As they ambled down the driveway to Nick's car parked at the curb, Mr. Griffiths yelled, "If you looked like that little buttercup, I might kiss you like that, Edie."

Chuckling, Nick opened the car door for her. "How about it…buttercup, do you want to stay here tonight?"

She filled her lungs with the salty air curling in from the ocean and shook her head. "I need Sunday to prepare for class the next day."

"And I told you, you're not going to class this week." He hunched over the car door, folding his arms across the top.

"Then I really need to do all the reading for the week on Sunday." She yanked the car door from beneath his arms and shut the door.

When this ended, once T.J. testified and the danger disappeared, she wanted to be ready. She wanted to be ready to gaze at Dr. Nick Marino from afar in the hospital and smirk at his exploits in the society pages. She wanted to steel her heart against any more of Nick's incursions. She didn't want to be disillusioned, disenfranchised and dumped.

She'd spent her entire adult life guarding against that kind of heartache, and just because Nick wanted her now didn't mean he'd want her later when the excitement had passed along with her usefulness to him.

He slid into the driver's seat and cranked the engine. "Do you still have time for lunch? I'm hungry, too, and I don't like anyone eating in this car." He smoothed his hand over the leather console, his jaw a hard line.

The man didn't take rejection well, but she'd already been too free and easy with her favors…sexual and every other kind. "Yeah, I have time for lunch. How about that place on the cliff with the patio?"

"Sounds good." Nick wheeled his perfect car onto the street, taking the turns to the restaurant overlooking the ocean in silence.

The breathtaking view and mile-high sandwiches did nothing to break through the sheet of cold glass between them. She breathed a long sigh of relief when Nick paid the bill, allowing her to leave the tip, and they hit the road again.

They drove for more than two hours, classical music from the CD player replacing all conversation. She preferred rock 'n' roll, but Nick didn't ask for her preferences.

She cleared her throat and took a sip of warm water from the bottle in the cup holder. "Do you need gas? I have to make a pit stop to use the bathroom."

"We have enough gas to get back to the city, but there's a rest stop coming up in about ten miles if you can hold on."

"That's fine. If there's a vending machine, do you want to get something to drink?" She shook the half-empty bottle of water. "This doesn't cut it."

He grunted a response. Pinning her hands between her knees, she gazed out the window at the fields of crops rushing by. Seemed if a woman didn't put out when Nick snapped his fingers, he cut her loose. If he thought she'd go down that road so easily, he had the wrong nurse.

Okay, so she'd already gone down that road, but he took advantage of her hysterical state. A killer had just attacked her and then the cops had grilled her while she continued to lie…for Nick's benefit. He'd seduced her to ensure her silence.

Nick finally turned down the music as he pulled into the empty parking lot of the rest stop, and Lacey jumped out of the car. "I'll be right back."

She strode toward the low-slung brown building that housed the restrooms, which had an overhang that covered a few picnic tables and a row of vending machines. After using the restrooms, she dumped some change out of her purse and bought two cans of soda. If Nick didn't want one, she'd drink both of them.

She headed back toward the car where Nick was lounging against the hood.

"My turn." He shoved off the car and loped across the scraggly grass to the back of the building and the men's restroom.

Lacey popped the lid of her soda, jerking her head up at the arrival of a blue sedan flying into the parking lot. Sheesh, did the guy think he was still on the highway?

He squealed to a halt two spaces over from Nick's car and flung the driver's side door open. A pair of light-colored slacks caught Lacey's eye, and she spun around to face the tall man from the service station bathroom.

And this time he had a gun.

Chapter Ten

Nick shredded the paper towel before he bunched it up and fired it into the trash can. Leaning against the sink, he stared into the wavy mirror at his distorted reflection. That's what Lacey saw when she looked at him—a monster with a criminal family, a violent background and a half life of secrets and lies.

Why would she be interested in getting any closer to him? She had a normal, stable life…or at least she did before she stumbled into his path.

A screech of tires disturbed the quiet of the rest stop, and Nick's pulse picked up speed. He pulled his gun out of his waistband where he'd shoved it when he got out of the car. Dangling his weapon at his side, he slipped out of the bathroom and crept toward the edge of the squat building.

He peered around the corner, and his heart stopped. A man had his arm pinned around Lacey's chest and a gun pointed at her head. Lacey squirmed and struggled in his grasp, while the man shouted something.

Running his tongue along his dry bottom lip, Nick released the safety on his .45. The guy wouldn't kill Lacey. He'd made that mistake three times before, and she represented his last hope of getting information about T.J.'s identity.

But he would abduct her.

Lacey screamed as the man dragged her toward the open door of his car. Nick vaulted from his hiding place, shooting into the air above their heads.

Startled, the man stumbled against his car door and Lacey broke free from his grip and rolled beneath Nick's car. When the killer recovered his balance, he swung his weapon in Nick's direction and fired back. As Nick lunged behind the little building, the bullet smacked the corner and a chunk of brown stucco flew past his face.

He poked his head out, shooting at the man now scrambling into his car. Nick could see Lacey flat on the ground underneath the BMW, and he prayed she'd stay there.

The killer's car roared to life and rolled past Nick's bumper. His weapon appeared at the window, and he fired at the ground, perilously close to Lacey's feet. As a truck barreled into the rest-stop parking lot, the man aimed one last shot toward the bathrooms and then peeled out of the parking lot, zigzagging back onto the freeway.

The adrenaline raging through Nick's body propelled him out to the parking lot like a rocket. He fell onto his knees next to the car, and then ducked underneath the chassis, arms outstretched to pull Lacey out.

Sobbing, she grasped his hand, and he yanked her across the oil-spattered asphalt. He rose to his knees, hauling her along with him. Locking her into an embrace, he ran his hands along her back to soothe the tremble that rolled down her spine.

A crunch of gravel behind them made them both jump.

The truck driver, a cap pulled low on his forehead, scratched his chin. "Everything okay? Was that guy in the blue car wavin' a gun out the window?"

Nick stood up, shielding Lacey's tear-streaked face from the truck driver's view. He obviously hadn't heard the gunshots.

"No shots fired. He's all bluff. The gun probably wasn't even loaded." Nick rolled his eyes. "Ex-boyfriend situation. The guy goes ballistic every time he sees her with another man."

"Dumb-ass." The truck driver shook his head. "When a woman says it's over, it's over. He's going to get hisself killed flashin' a gun like that."

He tromped over the grass toward the bathrooms, and Nick hustled Lacey into the car. He tossed the abandoned soda that lay fizzing on the ground into the trash, and dropped the other one into the cup holder. Then he stashed his gun beneath his seat. He hoped that truck driver wouldn't look too closely at the shattered piece of stucco or start combing the grass for bullets.

He maneuvered the car back onto the highway as another sob escaped Lacey's lips.

"Have some soda." He snapped the lid and the caramel-colored liquid foamed over the top, rushing down the sides of the can and pooling in the cup holder.

"Oh, Nick. Your beautiful car." She buried her face in her hands while her shoulders shook.

He knew she wasn't that upset about his car. "It's all right, Lacey. It's all over. You're safe now."

Her head popped up, and she rubbed her hands across her face, smearing tears and dirt in every direction. "How did he find us? It was the same man from the gas station, Nick. He must've followed us from San Francisco, but how?"

"I don't know." He pointed to the glove box. "There are some tissues in there."

She plucked several tissues from the box and mopped up the soda spill. He grabbed her wrist. "For your face, not the damn car."

She dropped the soggy tissues into the empty bag from the convenience store and grabbed a few more for her face. "He can't know I'm at that hotel. He would've tried something there."

"Maybe with all the snooping he's been doing, he knows about the doctor's beach house."

"And what? He waited on the side of the 101 Freeway until he saw us come by?"

Nick chewed his lip. "Someone clued him in that we were going."

"But nobody knew that except..."

"Dr. Buonfoglio's daughter."

"She wouldn't give that information to a stranger." Lacey twisted her hair into a knot behind her head, and then knotted her hands in her lap.

"Maybe not to a stranger."

"Are you saying Sarah knows this...this...gangster?"

"She wouldn't know him as a gangster." He ran his palms along the steering wheel, warming to his theory. "He could have introduced himself as a friend or a colleague."

She snorted. "Yeah, that guy really looks like a surgeon— a surgeon with a chainsaw, maybe."

She shivered and Nick rubbed the goose bumps on her arm. "A pharmaceutical salesman, whatever."

"That still doesn't explain how he tracked us to the service station or the rest stop."

Nick wanted to believe anything other than that the killer knew who he was and where he lived. That thought filled him with a cold dread. "What did he say to you back at the rest stop, Lacey?"

She took a gulp of soda, and then pressed the can against her cheek. "He told me he was going to take me to a nice, quiet place so I could remember where Dr. Buonfoglio hid all his files on the faces he cut. Told me he'd help me remember."

She squeezed her eyes shut and took another swallow of soda. "Nick, I asked him how he knew Dr. B had any files at all. That maybe Dr. B never kept files on those patients, and that no evidence or proof existed."

"What'd he say?"

"He said he knew the doc had those files." Her eyes flew open. "He used them to blackmail his patients to get more money out of them."

The sour spiral of anxiety in Nick's gut twisted tighter and he uttered a curse. T.J. never told him that part of the agreement with Dr. Buonfoglio. Even more reason why T.J. should've let him do the surgery.

"That ups the ante, doesn't it?" He massaged his temple.

"What do you mean?"

"If the De Lucas get their hands on that information, more people than just my brother will be in danger. The De Lucas could sell that information to other crime families, other gangs."

Her eyes widened. "Then we have to find the files before the De Lucas do, even after your brother testifies."

"There is no we, babe." He squeezed her stiff shoulder. "You're done. You're getting out of San Francisco until this is over."

"I told you, class starts this week. If I can't attend, I have to at least be around to do the assignments." She pursed her lips in a stubborn scowl.

"You're not going to do your patients much good if you're...hurt. I'll talk to May Pritchard for you. She can give you an extension on the work. Go visit your father in Florida or something."

"You're kidding."

"You said you had a half brother and sister you barely know." He lifted a shoulder. "Why punish them for your father's bad behavior? They might be suffering the same anxieties you suffered with him. Family's important, Lacey. I'd give anything to see my brother's ugly mug again."

"Your brother's not ugly." She hunched over and dug through her purse, suddenly finding something at the bottom of it fascinating.

His brows shot up. "And you know this how, other than the fact that he's called Pretty Boy?"

She looked up, her face flushed. "I did a little research on the Internet. I saw his picture."

"Had to check out my story, huh?"

"Of course. If I'm going to jump headfirst into the criminal life, I want to know all the details. And although your brother's mug is not as handsome as yours, he's one hot good fella."

Nick laughed, and it felt good. Even if Lacey wanted nothing to do with him when this situation came to its crashing crescendo, he'd enjoy what little time he had left with her.

"Everyone called T.J. 'Pretty Boy' because of his gleaming golden hair and designer suits." He swerved onto a ramp leading into Gilroy.

"The taste for designer suits must run in the family. Where are we going?"

"We're making a pit stop. I need some of those flaming-hot corn chips and another soda, since you drank mine, and you need to clean up. You look like hell." He reached over and plucked a twig sticking out of the top of her shirt.

"Thanks, I forgot my designer clothing."

He grinned, but a feather of fear brushed the back of his neck. He touched a dark smudge on her cheek. "This time, I'm not letting you out of my sight."

TWO DAYS AFTER THE ill-fated road trip, Lacey stretched out on the hotel bed and traced the purple bruise on her right knee. She sported a matching one on her left knee. Both represented badges of honor as she slipped out of a killer's grasp, slammed to the asphalt and scrambled beneath Nick's Beemer.

When she recognized the man from the service station getting out of the car at the rest stop and saw the gun pointing at her, she'd frozen. Her survival instinct didn't kick in until the guy had her in a vice grip. Then she struggled like a fish on a hook, with just about the same success, until Nick appeared out of nowhere with his gun blazing.

She didn't even know he had his gun with him, but it saved her life. Nick saved her life. The De Lucas' thug intended to squeeze information out of her...one way or another. Would she have folded? Told him about the key? Implicated Nick?

She drew up her bruised knees and wrapped her arms around her legs. She was glad she hadn't had the opportunity to find out.

Her cell phone rang, and she checked the display before answering it—restricted number. She licked her lips. "Hello?"

"Hi, Lacey, this is Sarah Jackson."

"Hi, Sarah." Lacey swallowed. She hoped those nosy Griffiths hadn't reported any suspicious behavior to Sarah.

"Did you get into Dad's house okay the other day?"

"Yeah, we did, thanks." All the disappointment of not finding the files came rushing back, although at the time that was the least of their worries.

"I'm going down to Santa Cruz this afternoon to pick up Abby. Do you want to come with me?"

Lacey stretched her legs out and wiggled her toes. Nick had been her constant companion for the past two days, but today he was performing an important surgery for a child flown in from Iraq.

Surely she could leave the hotel for one day—if she wore a disguise.

She needed a visit with sweet Abby more than anything right now. Dr. B's secret life, the blackmailing and the entire deception felt like a betrayal of their friendship, or at least of their professional relationship. He'd let her down, but he hadn't abandoned Abby.

"Yes, I'd like to see Abby before you take her back to Jersey. What time are you leaving?"

"In about an hour and a half. Can you meet me at Dad's office? I'm here right now packing up a few things."

Lacey sucked in her bottom lip. Was it safe to go back to the medical center? "Can you pick me up, Sarah?"

"Honey, I can't do that. I'm pressed for time as it is. I have to leave straight from the office."

"Okay, I'll be there in less than an hour."

When she ended the call, Lacey bounded up from the bed and threw open the closet door. Luckily springtime rain was still falling on the city. She yanked a black trench coat from a hanger in the closet and pulled a matching hat out of the pocket.

After she dressed in jeans, a green sweater and black boots, she shrugged into the coat, cinching the waist with the belt. She wrapped her hair on top of her head and shoved the hat over it, pulling the brim low on her forehead.

She faced her reflection in the mirror, winding a green scarf around her neck and pulling it over the bottom half of her face. That should do the trick, and now she knew her attacker's face. But he also knew her car, so she walked two blocks and hopped onto a bus that deposited her across the street from the medical offices.

Stepping off the bus, Lacey unfurled her umbrella against the light rain and hunched beneath it—indistinguishable from any other commuter on her way to work.

Without removing her rain gear, she waited in the lobby for a full elevator up from the parking garage and studied each face before she stepped into the car.

When Lacey got to the fifth floor, she noted that Sarah had propped open the office door and ordered a trash bin from facilities. Lacey poked her head inside the office and called, "Sarah?"

Sarah, short, plump and with energy to spare, came in from the back, wiping her hands on a paper towel. "Lacey? Is that you under all those clothes?"

"Yeah, it's wet out there." Lacey snatched the hat off her head and shook out her hair.

Sarah scurried forward and gave her a perfume-scented hug. "It's good so see you, honey. Too bad it's under these circumstances."

"I'm so sorry, Sarah." She hugged Sarah back, keeping a lid on all the sordid details she'd discovered about her father. "Has Detective Chu given you any hope that they'll catch your father's killer?"

"No." She wiped a tear from her face. "But he did tell me you were attacked in the parking structure and are still in danger. What are the police doing about that?"

Lacey lifted a shoulder weighed down by guilt. The SFPD might make more progress if she and Nick told them everything, but Nick didn't trust the police and he certainly didn't trust the FBI.

"I'm not a material witness to the case." She continued to climb into the black hole of deception. "I didn't see the man's face. I can't identify him, so the police can't offer protective custody."

"That's crap." Sarah wedged her hands on generous hips. "Is that the reason behind the get-up?" She waved a hand at Lacey's trench coat still buttoned up to her neck.

"Yeah, good disguise, huh?"

"It works. Before we take off, I have to deliver some papers to building security."

"Go ahead. I'll wait here for you." Lacey loosened her belt and slumped in a chair by the door. She had no desire to look around the office again.

Someone tapped on the open door, and Petra stuck her head around the corner. "Lacey, you're back."

"I'm here with Dr. B's daughter. We're taking off in a few minutes." Lacey continued to slouch in the chair, making no move to welcome Petra into her confidence.

Petra didn't need any excuse. She curled around the open doorway and rested a hand on the back of Lacey's chair. "I heard about the attack on you in the parking garage…and Dr. Marino's valiant rescue."

"Yeah, it was pretty scary." Lacey crossed her legs at the ankle and tapped her boots together. "Luckily, Dr. Marino and some people came off the other elevator and scared the guy off."

"Don't lean too heavily on Dr. Marino. He's a short-term kind of guy."

"Whatever." She'd like to wipe that smug look off Petra's face by telling her just how much she could count on Nick.

"You don't need him, anyway." Petra snapped her fingers. "There are plenty of men out there who appreciate a good woman. I met a fantastic guy last week—someone who's grateful for a home-cooked meal, companionship and conversation."

"Congratulations, Petra." Lacey shoved out of the chair and grabbed her hat.

"Do you want to see a picture of him? He's camera-shy, but I snapped him with my cell phone and he didn't even know it."

"Sure." Once this poor guy got a whiff of Petra's desperation and a taste of her infatuation for her boss, he'd disappear faster than Houdini. She may as well humor Petra while she still had a picture to show off.

Petra reached into the pocket of her smock and pulled out

her cell phone. She flipped it open and held it out for Lacey to see. "Isn't he a hunk and a half?"

A sharp pain sliced through Lacey's skull and her hand fumbled to grab the back of the chair as she stared at the picture of Petra's new boyfriend...and Dr. B's killer.

Chapter Eleven

"Wh-where'd you meet him?" The room spun, and Lacey had to concentrate very hard to get the words past her thick tongue.

"Downstairs at Antonio's Deli." Petra's eyes narrowed as she studied Lacey's face and snapped her phone shut. "I know he's a little rough around the edges, but he has his own waste-management company and makes good money."

Just like Tony Soprano. Lacey shoved her hands in her pockets. She could end this right here and now. She could call Detective Chu and expose Petra's new boyfriend as the murderer. Maybe they'd find him, maybe not, but surely they'd identify him. And once they did, all roads would lead to the FBI.

How far would certain elements in the FBI go to stop T.J. from testifying? And Nick? Would the FBI discover his identity, too, and realize he'd been hiding evidence all this time?

"What's your boyfriend's name?"

"David Pierce."

Yeah, right. "Does David know where you work?"

"Of course." Petra frowned and dropped her phone back in her pocket. "He's even heard about Dr. Marino."

"Really? Did he ask you about him?" Lacey's heart thundered so hard, the fringe at the end of her scarf trembled.

"Why, do you think David needs plastic surgery? He may not be as handsome as Nick, but he's built like a brick wall." Petra gave an exaggerated shiver.

She'd be doing a lot more shivering once she discovered her boyfriend was a killer. "Petra, I don't want to burst your bubble, but David Pierce is just using you to get the inside scoop on Nick. That's why I was so shocked when I saw his picture. He's a reporter for one of the tabloids, and he tried to cozy up to me to get info about Nick."

"Are you kidding me?"

"I wish I were." Lacey held her breath. Petra cycled through men faster than Lance Armstrong in the Tour de France, always looking for a substitute for Nick.

"Maybe that's why he hasn't called in a few days—the rat bastard." Petra yanked her cell phone out of her smock again and clicked a few buttons. "There. I deleted him."

Lacey sucked in a breath. She could've used that picture to show Detective Chu once T.J. testified. "Did you tell him anything about Nick?"

Petra raised her eyes to the ceiling. "I may have mentioned that he lived in one of the Queen Annes on Broadway, and I pointed out his car once in the parking structure."

A huge weight pressed against Lacey's chest, and she could barely breathe. David, or whatever his name was, must've followed Nick's car to San Luis Obispo. "I hope you didn't dish any dirt."

"Nooo. I better get back to the office. I hope that jerk never calls me again. He had dirty fingernails, anyway."

"Petra, is Dr. Marino still in surgery?"

"Yes. Don't tell him, Lacey." Petra gripped her arm, French-tipped nails clawing the sleeve of her coat.

"I won't tell him anything, but I need to see him when he's

out of surgery. I have a few more files to give him before Dr. B's daughter closes up this office for good."

"He'll be in surgery for the next three hours." Petra released her grip and spun out the door, probably in search of her next victim.

Maybe the fake David gave Petra the third degree about Nick because Nick foiled his attack, or he wanted to use Nick to get to her, which worked in San Luis Obispo. He probably didn't have a clue about Nick's true identity.

At least she hoped not.

With trembling hands, she pulled her cell phone out of her purse and speed-dialed Nick's cell. "Nick, I know you're in surgery for the next three hours, but there's something important you need to know. The De Luca drone cozied up to Petra to grill her about you…probably just to get to me. I told Petra some story to make her dump the guy, and I think it worked. In the meantime, I'm going down to Santa Cruz with Sarah Jackson, Dr. B's daughter. I'll be back tonight."

"I'm sorry that took so long." Sarah bustled into the office and lifted two boxes from the floor. She gestured to another box, a key chain dangling from her fingers. "Can you get that one and then take the keys and lock the door?"

"Sure." Lacey shoved the box into the hallway with her foot and grabbed the keys from Sarah. As she locked the door, she noticed the key chain in the shape of an *R*. "This was your mother's key chain. Your father started using it after she died."

"I figured that when I saw the *R*. It was among Dad's personal effects the cops gave to me."

As Lacey spread the keys across her palm, she noticed the small silver one dangling from a chain. Nick had taken the duplicate from the necklace around Jill's neck.

"Do you mind if I take this key?" She held up the small key, pinching it between her fingertips. "I think it fits a cabinet in which your father stored some special patient files. The cabinet is locked, and I have to turn those files over to the referral doctor."

At least she'd tried to stick with the truth.

"Go ahead. Take what you need."

Lacey slipped the chain off the key ring and dropped it in her coat pocket. Then she wound her hair up and pulled the hat on her head.

Ten minutes later, she sat in the passenger seat of Sarah's rental car as Sarah navigated the rain-slicked streets toward the freeway.

Sarah kept up a steady stream of chatter that required just a few ums and aahs from Lacey, which allowed her to keep an eye on the rearview mirror. No blue sedan followed them, but then she and Nick didn't notice anyone following them to San Luis Obispo, either.

By the time they reached the end of the curvy highway that snaked through the Santa Cruz Mountains, Lacey had to massage her stiff neck. She suspected every car on the road of following them. When one passed too closely, she braced herself for a bump and an attempt to run them off the road.

"We're here." Sarah pulled into the parking lot in front of a sprawling complex of low-slung, Spanish-style buildings, with red-tiled roofs and bougainvillea creeping across trellises. Their heady fragrance did battle with the salty sea air from the ocean less than a mile down the street from the complex.

A hand-painted sign greeted them at the entrance, and Lacey read it aloud. "Welcome to SLO, where every life is valued." She wrinkled her nose. "That's nice, but did we make a wrong turn or something? We're in Santa Cruz, not San Luis Obispo."

"Oh, SLO doesn't stand for San Luis Obispo. It's the name of the group home, Secure Living Options." Sarah swung open the door and waved Lacey through.

Her pulse tripping, Lacey squeezed past Sarah. *SLO*. She'd assumed Dr. B's SLO notation in his calendar indicated his beach cottage. Now that she thought of it, that house smelled too musty and dank to have had recent occupants. Did SLO refer to Secure Living Options?

Sarah greeted the woman seated in the homey living room where a few residents were watching TV. "Hi, I'm Abby Buonfoglio's sister."

The woman rose and extended her hand. "I'm Cheryl Yardley. I'm so glad you're here, Mrs. Jackson. Abby's been asking about her father. She knows something's wrong because he visited her quite frequently."

"I'm not looking forward to telling her. I'm sorry, this is Lacey Kirk, a friend of the family."

The woman smiled. "Abby's mentioned you several times. She said you two sang karaoke together."

Lacey laughed. "She really enjoyed it."

"When was that?" Raising her brows, Sarah tilted her head.

"When your mom had Abby home one weekend, she invited my mom and me over for dinner. Abby and I put on a show after dinner."

A corkscrew of pain twisted in her belly. Now three of those people at that happy dinner were dead, and she'd since discovered one was a blackmailer. When she remembered Dr. B's face shining with love and pride when Abby grabbed the microphone from her and sang a verse of the song, she could almost forgive him. He'd do anything for his daughter, which was more than she could say for her own father.

Cheryl asked, "Do you remember where Abby's room is? It's in the first building on the left when you exit this one, room twenty-six."

"Thanks, we'll find it."

They followed a flagstone path through lush gardens and past a gurgling fountain to the next building.

"This is a beautiful place." Lacey bent over to inhale the fragrance of a yellow rose. "Too bad you can't keep Abby here."

"Yeah, Dad must've performed a lot of surgeries to afford this home. I hope we can find something half as nice in Jersey."

"I don't mean to pry, Sarah, but did your dad leave you any money for Abby's care?"

"My husband, Craig, is going to handle that with my father's attorney. Seems Dad had a few offshore accounts." Her brow furrowed. "I don't know what that's all about. Probably just wanted to avoid taxes or something."

Or avoid the mob, the FBI and the IRS.

They found Abby's room, and Sarah tapped on the door. "Abby, it's Sarah."

The door swung open and Abby threw herself in her sister's arms. "I missed you, Sarah."

"I missed you, too, honey." She stepped back. "Look who came with me."

"Lacey!" Abby embraced her. "Do you want to sing?"

"Maybe later." Lacey stroked Abby's ponytail. "Your sister needs to talk to you."

"About Dad?" Abby turned to Sarah, who was dabbing her eyes with a tissue.

"Yes, honey, about Dad." She took her hand. "Do you want to go for a walk?"

Abby nodded.

"Is it okay if Lacey waits in your room?"

"Yes, Lacey can stay here." Abby broke away from Sarah and moved around the room, pointing out her drawings, pictures of her friends and her collections of odds and ends.

When the two sisters left the room, Lacey pulled the key out of her pocket and peeked behind the artwork hanging on the walls. Abby didn't have any file cabinets in her room, and her desk wasn't locked.

Lacey sat back on her heels, her gaze scanning the four walls and tracking back to the walk-in closet. She shoved up from the floor and swung open the closet door.

Abby's clothes hung in neat rows, and Lacey caught a whiff of potpourri. Dropping to her knees, she searched among shoes and accessories, feeling like a voyeur. As she stood up, her shoulder caught the hem of several dresses, which slid across the rack, exposing a glint of silver on the closet wall.

A rush of adrenaline pumped through her veins as she parted the dresses and discovered a safe built into the wall. Her breath hitched in her throat. With shaky fingers, she inserted the small key into the lock. It turned.

She eased the safe door open. A stack of files almost a foot high took up most of the space. She hoisted them out of the cavity, balancing them against her chest. Crouching to the floor, she glanced at the tab on the top file. It was a name, beginning with *A*.

She thumbed through the rest of the tabs and nearly dropped the entire pile when she read *Paglietti, T.J.* on one of the labels.

Voices echoed from the hallway outside Abby's door, and Lacey scrambled to her feet. She plucked T.J.'s file from the stack and shoved the rest back into the wall safe. She locked the safe, straightened Abby's clothes and stumbled out of the closet. As the door to Abby's room opened, Lacey stuck the file inside her coat and buttoned it to the top.

When Sarah and Abby walked into the room, Lacey was standing by the window. She hugged a tearful Abby, smoothing her hair back from her brow. "Are we still having lunch?"

"Of course." Sarah blew her nose. "Abby's taking us to her favorite restaurant on the boardwalk."

"In the rain?"

"It's not raining anymore, Lacey." Abby pointed to her wet cheeks. "Only from my eyes."

Lacey gave thanks to the cloudy skies—an excuse to keep her trench coat buttoned up. When they got to the restaurant, she dashed into a tourist shop next door and bought a book on the history of Santa Cruz. Before joining Sarah and Abby at the table, she slipped T.J.'s file from her coat and slid it into the bag from the store. She couldn't wait to sneak a peek, but she couldn't do it in front of Sarah.

Outside the restaurant, she called Nick's cell phone again, even though he'd be in surgery for another hour. This message couldn't wait. "Nick, I found the file. Your brother's going to be safe."

During lunch, Lacey didn't hear a word of conversation, didn't taste a bite of the fish and chips she consumed, didn't see the gray ocean with its white caps or smell its tangy scent. The frightening truth overpowered all her senses.

T.J.'s brother might be safe, but she was holding a stick of dynamite.

NICK PEELED OFF HIS surgical mask and gloves and dropped them in the bin on his way out of the operating room. Greg, one of his surgical nurses, followed him out. "Great work, Dr. Marino. You do a lot of good for those kids."

"Couldn't have done it without you, Greg." He slapped him on the back and rounded the corner to his office. A pile of messages awaited him on his desk, and his cell phone beeped insistently. Still wearing scrubs, he collapsed in his chair and thumbed through the messages.

Nothing too urgent. He flipped open his cell phone, hoping to hear a message from Lacey telling him she'd booked her flight to Florida. She'd promised him she'd try to get a flight out tomorrow.

He skipped through three messages, and kicked his feet up on his desk when he heard Lacey's voice on the fourth. But when he heard the message, he almost fell back in his chair.

Damn Petra. He had the wrong person when he suggested to Lacey that the De Lucas' thug would pose as someone else to get information from Dr. Buonfoglio's daughter.

And damn Lacey. She should've been making flight reservations instead of running off to Santa Cruz.

Without listening to his remaining voice mail, he snapped his phone shut and buried his fingers in his hair.

The man knew where he lived. He could pick out his car. Had he been watching the house? Had he dug any deeper? How had he known about the trip to San Luis Obispo if he hadn't followed them? He hadn't told Petra about that.

He jumped up from his chair and scooped his car keys out of his jacket pocket. As he strode through the office toward the back door, Zoe called out, "Do you want me to order you some lunch, Dr. Marino?"

He waved at her, and then bypassing the elevators, he jogged down six flights of stairs to the parking garage. He pressed his remote as he approached his car to disable the alarm. Then he crouched behind it, reaching beneath the chassis to run his hand along the inside of the frame.

His fingers tripped over an object slightly smaller than a TV remote control, and he pried the magnetic device off the car. A red light blinked on the oblong box—a tracking device. The killer didn't have to be right behind them. He could follow them from several miles back.

When did the guy attach this to his car? Here in the parking garage or at his house?

He leaned against the trunk of his car and called Aunt Paula. Thank God she'd left for her home in Stinson today. Her answering machine picked up, so he tried her cell phone. His heart stuttered when she didn't answer her cell, either. Must be out with her cell phone off or maybe she couldn't hear it.

He popped open his trunk and dragged out the tire iron. Looking both ways, he ducked behind a cement pillar and dropped the tracking device to the garage floor. Then he smashed it with the tire iron.

Take that, you bastard.

He placed the tire iron back in the car and chucked the mangled tracking device into a trash can in the garage. Then he returned to his office to shower and change. He'd stay here until Lacey returned from Santa Cruz. They could look at the file together.

He settled behind his desk to review the photos of the next child coming from a country in need. The office door opened and he glanced up, scowling at Zoe, who hovered on the threshold. This better be good.

"Excuse me, Dr. Marino. There's been an accident."

"An accident?" Nick's heart hammered in his chest as he clutched the edge of his desk.

"The highway patrol just called. Your aunt's car went off a cliff on Highway 1."

They knew. The De Lucas had discovered Dominick Paglietti.

"How bad is it? Is she…?"

Zoe spread her hands. "I'm sorry, I don't know anything more, but the officer left his number."

He snatched the paper from her outstretched hand. When Zoe left his office, he grabbed the phone and punched in the number she'd scribbled on the note.

A man answered, "Officer Rodriguez."

"Officer, this is Dr. Nick Marino. You called about my aunt. She was in an accident on Highway 1." His legs felt like rubber, so he perched on the edge of his desk.

"Yes, Dr. Marino. It was pretty bad. Her car plunged over the side and down an embankment. She's alive but in a coma, so we're not sure what happened. From the dents on the rear of her car, it looks like another car was involved, but it left the scene."

"And my niece? How's my niece?"

"Your niece?"

The blood pounded in Nick's temples, and he wedged a clammy palm on his desk. "A five-year-old girl, she was in the car with my aunt."

"I guess that's the silver lining. Your aunt was alone. There was no child in the car."

Chapter Twelve

Sarah pulled the car to the side of the road as the ambulance zoomed by, sirens blaring. "Looks like there was an accident."

Lacey smoothed her hands over the bag from the board-walk shop, currently burning a hole through her slacks right down to her thighs. She pulled her cell phone out and sent another text message to Nick. Where was he? He had to be out of surgery by now.

"Are you okay, Lacey? You've been distracted ever since lunch."

"I'm sorry. I have a lot on my mind."

"Well, you go ahead and make that phone call."

"No, it's all right. I've left him enough messages. He'll call when he's able." Lacey chewed her lip. Was Nick able? He put himself right in the line of fire by thwarting three attacks on her. He gave himself the visibility that he'd wanted to avoid with the De Lucas—all to protect her. The De Lucas went as far as infiltrating Nick's office to get information about him. How much more would they discover about the heroic Dr. Nick Marino?

As they entered the city, Sarah asked, "Do you want me to drop you off at your house? I have to go back to Dad's office to pick up the rest of the boxes."

"I'll come with you. The person I've been trying to call is in the same building."

"A doctor?" Sarah's eyebrows shot up to the bangs of her carefully styled hair. "I never thought you'd date a doctor, girl. Therapy?"

Lacey grimaced. *No, just a couple of murderous attacks.*

When they arrived at the office, Lacey reluctantly dropped the plastic bag containing the book on Santa Cruz and T.J. Paglietti's new identity into her desk drawer and locked it. She then helped Sarah haul two boxes down to Shipping and Receiving, so Sarah could ship them off to New Jersey.

She said her goodbyes to Sarah at the elevator, promising to visit Abby until Sarah could return with her husband to move her to Jersey. Then she rushed back up to the fifth floor. Her steps faltered outside of Nick's office.

Why hadn't he returned her calls and messages? He must've had consultations immediately after surgery. She'd give it one more try. He deserved to be the first one to get a look at his brother's new face. She owed him that.

She pushed open the door to Nick's office and halted at the threshold, startled by the empty waiting room. Nick usually entertained a packed house.

Zoe looked up. "Hi, Lacey. Did you hear the news?"

A spiral of fear twisted in her belly. Had her message this morning about Petra's new boyfriend come too late? Swallowing and gripping the door handle behind her, Lacey shook her head.

"Dr. Marino's aunt was in a car accident. She's in a coma."

"Oh, no." The door slipped out of Lacey's grasp and slammed shut as she sank to the nearest chair. This couldn't possibly be a coincidence. He knew. "What about Miranda?"

"Who's Miranda?"

Lacey gripped her hands together. She'd forgotten. Nobody knew about Miranda. "She's his niece."

"He didn't mention a niece, and neither did the highway patrol officer who called." Zoe frowned, and Lacey got the impression she was wondering how the hell Lacey Kirk knew so much about Dr. Marino and his family.

Lacey filled her lungs with air and straightened her shoulders. Thank God Miranda was okay.

Zoe swept her arm across the room. "I canceled all his appointments for the rest of the day. He drove out to the hospital where they took her."

"It didn't happen in the city?"

"No, somewhere out by Highway 1, near Stinson Beach."

Lacey niggled her bottom lip. If Nick's aunt was on her way home, why didn't she have Miranda with her?

"If you hear from Dr. Marino, please tell him to call me when he gets the chance." She stood up and opened the door. "I have one last, very important file to turn over to him before I vacate Dr. Buonfoglio's office completely."

"Will do."

Lacey rushed down the hall to Dr. B's office. Guess she'd be the first to see the new-and-improved T.J. Her hands shook so much, it took several tries for her to get the key in the lock. She slammed the door behind her and secured the dead bolt. She pushed through the swinging door to her office space, unlocked her desk drawer and let out a long sigh when she grabbed the bag, the plastic crinkling between her fingers.

She slid the folder out of the bag with clammy hands and flipped open the cover. She shuffled through the standard paperwork—intake form, medical history, pre-op instructions—until she got to the photos in the back of the file.

She pulled out the first side-by-side before-and-after picture and dropped the folder to the floor where the rest of the papers scattered. With her mouth hanging open, she brought the photo close to her face and blinked her eyes.

Then the picture slipped from her fingers and the world went black.

NICK DRAGGED A CHAIR next to his aunt's hospital bed and tucked her cold hand in his. He whispered, "I'm sorry, Aunt Paula, but you're going to pull through. You have to pull through." He leaned in closer, his lips brushing her ear. "Where's Miranda?"

When the California Highway Patrol officer told him on the phone that there was no child in the car, Nick had felt as if someone had slammed the back of his head with a sledge-hammer. He knew, even if the cops didn't, that whoever ran his aunt off the road had also grabbed his niece.

Of course, he couldn't tell any of this to the police. He knew how to play the game. Hell, he'd played the game during his formative years to cover for his father.

Omerta.

He had to follow the code of silence—not to protect the scum who'd taken his niece and threatened his brother—but to save them both. If he told the police the same man who caused the accident had kidnapped Miranda, she would pay with her life.

He had to get her back on his own, and as much as the fury singed every nerve ending in his body, he had to play the waiting game. The De Lucas would make the first move.

A nurse entered the room. "Dr. Marino, the police would like to talk to you again before they leave."

He hesitated, squeezing his aunt's hand.

The nurse smiled. "Don't worry. We'll take good care of your aunt."

Nick thanked her and stepped into the hallway where two

uniformed CHP officers waited. "How's your aunt doing, Dr. Marino?"

"She's still in a coma, but her doctors are hopeful she'll come out of it."

"We have a lot of questions for her." The officer flipped through a notebook. "There were no witnesses to the accident, but we're sure a second car was involved as there were dents and scratches on the rear of the car and some streaks of blue paint."

The bastard must still be driving the blue sedan. "Who reported the accident?"

"A motor officer spotted the car down the embankment and called it in. Scared the hell out of us when we saw the child car seat in the back."

"The car seat was in the back?" Nick formed the words with dry lips, a muscle ticking in his jaw.

"Yeah, but we did a search of the area for a child and thank God we didn't find one. You did locate your niece, didn't you?"

"She's with a relative." Nick ran the back of his hand across his mouth. The killer must've snatched Miranda before Aunt Paula's car went over the edge. His goal was to kidnap Miranda, not kill her...not yet, anyway.

Nick crossed his arms over his chest, bunching his fists into his biceps to keep from smashing one of them into the wall.

He had to wait for the demands, but he had nothing to give them. He and Lacey hadn't found the files. He had no better idea of what his brother looked like than the De Lucas did. Would they believe him or would they hold on to Miranda until he found out?

"Let us know when your aunt regains consciousness, Dr. Marino." The officer held out his card. "We can't release her car yet as this is an on-going investigation."

By the time Nick looked in on his aunt again, spoke to her

doctors and made arrangements to have her moved to SF General, the night sky loomed dark and starless.

He slumped in his car and flicked on the dome light. He'd been so busy since getting the news about Aunt Paula, he hadn't had time to finish checking his messages. And it was very important that he check his messages…a matter of life and death.

How would the De Lucas contact him? They'd most likely call his office since all his other numbers were unlisted. Would they leave a message with his exchange, or would he have to wait until tomorrow to get word about Miranda?

Maybe they'd show up at his house.

He put his cell phone on speaker and punched in the code to retrieve his voice mail. Lacey's voice, clear and excited, filled the car. "Nick, I found the file. Your brother's going to be safe."

Lacey just gave him the means to rescue Miranda.

He dropped his head, wedging his brow against the steering wheel. T.J. would never be safe now. Nick had to sacrifice his brother to save his brother's daughter.

He scanned the rest of the voice-mail messages and clicked through several text messages, all from Lacey. He deleted everything and then called Lacey's cell. As long as she had that file, she was in danger. He had to think. He had to formulate a plan. He had to get that file from her.

On the drive home, his brain whirred and clicked through different scenarios. He could falsify the information. Use a record from his own practice and pass it off as T.J.'s. Rescue Miranda without turning over anything.

He pounded the steering wheel. He'd failed his brother, succeeding only in living the good life as T.J. ordered.

When he'd graduated from medical school, T.J. came to see him. He took Nick by the shoulders and said, "I have to live my life underground, but you don't. Make the most of it. Live it up for me."

And he had.

Nick jumped headfirst into the life of the carefree bachelor. The money, the clothes, the expensive neighborhood, the women, the glittering social scene were all supposed to avenge the Paglietti family—his father lost to him, his brother on the lam and his mother dead.

He played that role to a T, but he bombed at the important part—protecting what little family he had left. Now Aunt Paula lay in a coma, and some low-life thug had Miranda.

His gut constricted and sour bile convulsed in his chest. If that guy laid a hand on her or frightened her, he'd kill him.

When he pulled into his driveway, he grabbed the gun out of his briefcase and released the safety. Then he slid his cell in his front pocket.

As he reached the porch steps, a figure moved out of the shadows. He spun around, leveling the gun in front of him. The waxy glow from the porch light illuminated Lacey's face, a white oval framed by loose, dark hair.

Her eyes flicked from the gun to his face and he eased his finger off the trigger, blowing out a long breath.

"Are you going to shoot me now, you lying bastard?"

NICK DROPPED THE GUN to his side. With his mouth open, he glanced over his left shoulder as if to make sure she wasn't talking to someone hovering behind him.

In the weak light his face appeared drawn, and the dark smudges beneath his eyes gave them a hollow look.

Screw the sympathy. She hugged the plastic bag to her chest where her heart thumped a painful staccato beat. If he got her message about the file, he just might shoot her. But before he did, she'd kick up such a fuss, all his upscale neighbors would rush outside…or at least call the cops from behind closed doors.

"What the hell are you talking about?" He gripped her upper arm and yanked her toward the front door. "It's dangerous out here. The De Lucas know where I live. Our friend put a tracking device on my car. My aunt's in a coma and Miranda's been kidnapped."

That last one got her—sucked all the rage right out of her body. She doubled over, tripping on the step.

Nick threw open the door and shoved her inside. "You're the one who told me about Petra's new flame. You should have more sense than to show up on my doorstep unannounced. Did you at least bring my brother's file with you?"

She held her head with both hands, shaking it back and forth. Had he dipped into his drug supplies? "Back up a minute. What happened to Miranda?"

"When De Lucas' hit man ran my aunt off the road, he took Miranda."

"Oh…Nick." She covered her face and collapsed on the sofa. Whatever he did, whatever he lied about, the misery in his voice echoed in every word he spoke. How could these animals take a little girl? "Has anyone contacted you?"

"Not yet, but they will."

"Let me guess. You didn't tell the police about the kidnapping."

"And sign Miranda's death warrant? No, I didn't tell the cops." He sat next to her, hunching forward on the sofa.

She didn't have to ask what the De Lucas' demands would be. In fact, they'd have only one demand, and it rested in her lap. "What are you going to do, Nick? If you give them what they want, you'll sign your own death warrant."

"What do you mean?" His brows collided over his nose. "They'll kill my brother. They're not interested in me beyond what I can give them…my brother's identity."

"Nick, it's over. You don't need to lie to me anymore." She

pulled the file out of the bag and dropped it on the coffee table. "I didn't wait for you. I already looked at the files. I saw the pictures."

"And?"

"Cut the crap." She flipped open the folder and fanned the contents out on the table. Pressing a fingertip on the before-and-after photo of T.J. Paglietti, she dragged it from the pile and pinched the corner between two fingers.

She dangled the picture in front of Nick's face. "Just like looking in a mirror, right, T.J.?"

Chapter Thirteen

Nick peered at the photos through a fog of confusion. His brother's face on the left…and his face on the right.

He snatched the picture from Lacey's hand and stumbled into the kitchen. He flicked on the lights over the granite island and slapped the photo down on the counter. With a dull pain grinding against the base of his skull, he traced over the two faces with his fingertips.

Gripping the picture, he swung around and collided with Lacey hovering behind him. He shook the picture at her. "You think this is me? You think I'm T.J., and I've been handing you a line of bull ever since I saved your pretty little ass from that killer?"

She stepped back, her green eyes wide and glassy. "B-but that *is* you."

He smacked the picture down and Lacey jumped. He didn't know what cut him more—that Lacey believed he'd lied to her or that his brother had used his face. "Are you so afraid to trust, you'd allow that fear to blind you to common sense?"

"You were desperate to find that file and keep the police out of it." She clasped her hands over her stomach, her knuckles white. "When I saw that picture—"

"You jumped to an insane conclusion." He clawed at his

hair, moving several paces away from her. "Do you really believe a criminal in hiding from both the mob and the feds would up and decide to attend medical school?"

"I don't know how the Witness Protection Program works. There might be dentists, vets and accountants out there, all with new identities." She snagged her bottom lip between her teeth, a tide of crimson rushing into her cheeks.

Did she finally realize how ludicrous that sounded? He had to make sure. He wanted her back on his side.

He brushed past her, threw open a cupboard door and lifted a key from a hook on the inside. He strode across the room and crouched before a black lacquered cabinet. Inserting the key into a small door, he unlocked it and pulled out a photo album.

On his way back to the kitchen, he grabbed Lacey's hand and pulled her along behind him. He plopped the album onto the counter and flipped through the pages.

Jabbing his finger at photo after photo, he said, "Here's a picture of me and my brother at the Jersey shore. Here's one of us in Atlantic City. Here we are in the snow in front of our apartment building. Two of us. Two different Paglietti boys— one blond, one dark."

She folded her arms on the countertop and buried her head in the crook of her elbow, her shoulders shaking.

"You have to believe me, Lacey." He rubbed a hand along the curve of her back. He'd never trusted a woman with so much of himself, never wanted to.

"I believe you, Nick." She twisted her head to the side, strands of hair clinging to her tear-streaked face.

With his fingertip, he swept the strands behind her ear, lingering on her soft earlobe. She nestled her face against his palm. "Why'd he do it? Why'd your brother change his appearance to look like you?"

"I don't know." His gut knotted into a ball of pain. Maybe T.J. resented him all these years, resented his freedom and his lifestyle and wanted revenge. Nick didn't blame him, couldn't condemn him.

Straightening up, she caressed his face with her hands, smoothing the pads of her thumbs between his eyebrows. "He didn't know, Nick. He didn't realize Dr. B was going to give him your face. He saved your life. He protected you all these years, and wouldn't even involve you by going to you for his surgery. He wouldn't betray you."

"I don't know, Lacey." He kissed her palm for trying to make him feel better. "I don't know my brother anymore. He lived on the edges of society for years before snagging that job for the De Lucas and then testifying against them."

"If he went that far to avenge your mother's death, he wouldn't give up his own brother...the brother he saved and protected."

The knot in his belly loosened. He wanted to believe her. "Why would Buonfoglio change my brother's face to look like mine?"

"I'm not sure. I know he envied your thriving practice." She shrugged. "Why did he do any of the things he did?"

"Money. I'm sure the criminals paid him well, and then the good doctor made sure they'd pay again and again by keeping their files and threatening blackmail."

"That's it!" She snapped her fingers. "He figured he could get even more money out of T.J. if the identity he turned over to the De Lucas was yours, putting you in danger."

He shook his head. "As wonderful as that all sounds, I'm not sure. But if it's true, Dr. Buonfoglio did me a favor."

"Exactly how did he do you a favor by duplicating your face on a witness on the run from the FBI and some lunatic crime family?"

He swept the photo from the counter and clasped it to his chest. "Because now I can save my brother *and* his daughter."

"HOW IS THAT PHOTO GOING to save T.J. and Miranda?" She stared into his dark eyes, flat and opaque with the look of fatalism, and her heart shuddered. "No, Nick."

"It's poetic justice."

"It's insanity. You're going to turn yourself over to the De Lucas, hand them this file and pretend to be T.J. It'll never work."

"Of course it will. Once they see the before-and-after photo and realize they have T.J. Paglietti in their clutches, they'll release Miranda."

"And then they'll see T.J. show up at that federal courthouse to testify against Big Jimmy, and realize they were duped." A cold fear rushed through her body like an avalanche. She couldn't allow him to sacrifice himself for his brother. She couldn't lose him.

"By then it will be too late. T.J. will have given his testimony against Big Jimmy and the FBI agents who were in bed with the De Lucas. The FBI will resettle him, and he can finally take Miranda with him and his wife, Cee Cee."

He placed the photo back in the file and arranged the rest of the papers in a neat stack, as if he weren't preparing his own execution order.

"There won't be enough time. T.J.'s coming in to testify in three days."

He looked at his watch. "I expect a call with their demands, if not tonight, then as soon as my office opens tomorrow morning. This can be a done deal tomorrow."

"They won't believe you." She had to keep grasping at straws to find the one that would break this crazy web of redemption he was weaving. Nick never got over the survival guilt of being the one Paglietti family member to escape that horrible day unscathed.

"Sure they will." He tapped his finger on the file. "I have the proof right here."

"It's like you told me, Nick. The De Lucas will never believe that a small-time hood turned into a top-notch cosmetic surgeon." Tears streamed down her face as she grabbed his bicep, as hard and unyielding as his resolve to repay T.J. for saving his life.

"The De Lucas aren't too bright. Besides, I can claim that Dr. Nick Marino is my brother, and I cut my face to look like his for sentimental reasons."

He finally turned to look at her, and his eyes lost the hard look that shot daggers of fear through her heart. He dabbed at a tear with his fingertip and held it under the light. "Don't cry, Lacey. I have to save my niece."

"I know that, but why can't you just tell the truth…for once? Give them the photos. Tell them your brother now looks exactly like you. Tell them you're Dr. Nick Marino. Tell them…" Her words ended on a sob as she beat her fists against Nick's chest.

He gathered her against his body and held her tightly. He whispered, "I wish, I wish…"

Her head fell against his shoulder, and she uncurled her hands and smoothed her palms against his granite chest. "Please, Nick. Oh, God, I love you. I can't lose you."

"You have me, for tonight…for always." He groaned and captured her lips in a fiery kiss.

Then he swept her up in his arms and carried her upstairs. He kicked open the door to a darkly furnished masculine room that smelled of his spicy cologne and leather-bound medical texts and manly comfort and everything she'd always desired.

He undressed her quickly, frantically, as if she'd disappear, as if he'd never see her again. And she tugged at his clothes with a desire born of the notion that if she could just press her skin against his skin, if she could just overpower his senses with her love, he'd come back to reason and sanity.

They fell across the bed, naked in each other's arms. He devoured her with his lips and tongue, bringing her to pinnacles of desire she'd never experienced before. She soaked in every sensation, committing it to memory.

Then she pushed him back on the bed, straddling his hips. She dragged her fingers through his hair, brushing it back from his high forehead, then kissed his eyelids, the dark shadows beneath his eyes and his prominent cheekbones.

While she kissed his mouth, he dug his fingers into her bottom, lifting and urging her forward. Then he lowered her onto his erect shaft, filling and satisfying her need for him. She threw her head back and rode him, clamping her thighs against the corded muscle that ran along his hips.

His large hands encircled her waist, and he rolled over, taking the dominant position on top, driving into her again and again. Her need for him grew with every thrust, and she wound her legs around his thighs, urging him closer, urging him to give her everything.

He growled with the pleasure of his release and then kissed her mouth tenderly. Lacey exulted in the heavy weight of his body as it pressed against hers. She ran her tongue along his shoulder, savoring the salty, primal taste.

Sucking in her stomach, she willed his seed to stay inside her, to stay with her…even after he left.

THE FOLLOWING MORNING Nick laced his hands behind his head and stared at the ceiling while Lacey ran her fingers through the hair on his chest.

He couldn't do it. He couldn't leave her. In Lacey, he'd found everything he'd always wanted—a strong woman he could trust and count on, a woman who wouldn't fall apart when the insanity of his past life overwhelmed the present. Within his grasp, he had the opportunity to mold a new life for himself, one he'd dreamed of since the day his mother died.

"I have a plan."

She turned her head, her hair tickling his belly. "I've heard your plan. I don't like it."

He stroked her shoulder. "Same plan, different ending."

"Since that other ending is completely unacceptable, give me the new one."

"I trade myself for Miranda, telling the De Lucas I'm T.J. Then when Miranda's safe, you call the cops and the FBI. Maybe they can get there in time."

Her eyes widened, and she dug her nails into his chest. "So they can find your lifeless body sooner rather than later? How is that any better?"

"I'll stall the De Lucas. I'll cook up some story about an army of thugs ready to come to my rescue, or I'll tell them the dirty FBI agents are ready to testify against Big Jimmy."

"They're not going to buy that, Nick. Tell them the truth. Tell them you're not T.J., but that T.J. looks just like you now."

"I can't do that, Lacey. Don't you see? By some weird twist of fate, I've been given the opportunity to repay my brother for saving my life."

She sat up, gripping the sheet to her chest. "But T.J. didn't give his life for you, Nick. You're paying him back with way too much interest."

"He did give his life for me. My aunt plucked me out of that environment and left him there. He fell into the same mold as our father. Then he saw the opportunity to avenge our mother's death and testified against a capo in one of the biggest mob families in Jersey. He never would've done any of that if my aunt had taken him, too. He could've done something important with his life."

"He made his own choices." She took his face in her hands, smoothing her palms against his beard. "You don't owe him your life."

The cell phone he kept for work rang on the nightstand, and he grabbed it. "Hello?"

"Dr. Marino, this is the exchange. We have an urgent message for you."

"Go ahead." He scrambled for a pen and pad of paper in the drawer.

"The brother of your patient Jimmy Dee called and said his brother was having some complications from his surgery. He left a number and wants you to call immediately."

Nick's heart pounded and his pulse ramped up as he took down the number. *This is it.*

As he swung his legs over the side of the bed and felt the floor for his boxers, Lacey asked, "Is it him?"

"Yeah, it's him." He pulled on his underwear and perched on the edge of the bed while punching in the phone number.

The phone rang twice before a voice answered. "Yeah?"

"This is Dr. Nick Marino calling for Jimmy Dee's brother."

The man coughed and cleared his throat. "Yeah, right. You mean Dr. Dominick Paglietti."

"Yeah, I'm Dominick Paglietti." The muscles in Nick's back tensed as he hunched his shoulders.

Lacey ran her palm along his stiff spine. She knew what it cost him to utter those words. He'd been running from that identity for twenty years.

"Where's my niece?"

Lacey rolled off the bed and gathered her clothes as Nick kept talking.

Nick growled, "An even trade. I give you what you want, and you release her, unharmed."

He planned to go through with this deception, and she couldn't think of a damn thing to do to stop him.

By the time Nick had finished the conversation and scribbled some information on a pad of paper, Lacey had gotten dressed. She settled next to him on the bed. "Where do they have her? Is she okay?"

"Oh, no, you don't." He ripped the paper with the notes from the pad and folded it in half. "I'm meeting him at nine o'clock tonight. I heard Miranda's voice in the background, and she sounded fine."

Frowning, he ran a hand through his hair. Lacey asked, "What's wrong? Miranda's okay, isn't she?"

"I heard her talking to a woman."

"So? That's probably a good thing, isn't it? Better than having a bunch of goons looking after her."

"The man on the phone claimed to be Big Jimmy's brother, Frankie De Luca, and I've never heard of a family bringing a woman into the business." He pushed up from the bed and parted the heavy drapes, peering at the weak early morning sun, which made a valiant effort to throw a couple of beams of light onto the hardwood floor.

"Is that good or bad?"

"It's good, all good." He turned, wedging a shoulder against the window. "It means the De Luca family isn't behind this vendetta."

"You lost me. I thought the De Lucas engineered the hunt for T.J. to stop him from testifying against Big Jimmy again." She clapped a hand over her mouth and jumped up from the bed. "Do you mean the FBI kidnapped Miranda?"

He took her hands and kissed them. "No. I think Frankie

is acting on his own, without the backing of the De Luca family, and that's good news."

The thought of going up against one disgruntled family member instead of an entire mob family comforted her slightly more, but the man meant business. She'd been on the receiving end of his perseverance more than once. "How do you know for sure?"

"I don't know for sure, but hearing the woman's voice in the background with Miranda was another hint that the mob isn't behind this. Mob families do not use women in situations like this, and they don't normally kidnap children, either... even the De Lucas."

He shivered and hunched his shoulders. *They tried to kill him when he was a child.* She wrapped her arms around him, resting her chin on his shoulder. "Do you think you might be able to overpower him and take Miranda back?"

He rubbed his cheek against her head, the stubble of his beard catching strands of her hair. "I have to. I have someone to come home to now."

She squeezed tighter, molding her body to his. A black fear engulfed her. After all her careful planning and precautions, she'd fallen for a man destined to leave her, anyway.

DANGER NO LONGER STALKED Lacey for the first time in two weeks, but she felt more bereft than at any time in her life.

Nick left for his office in the morning as if he didn't have an appointment with death in the evening. Lucky for him he didn't have any surgeries today, but he probably could have pulled off one or two face-lifts. The man had nerves of steel.

He told her to meet him at his place tonight so he could give her instructions to pick up Miranda when Frankie De Luca released her. And to say goodbye?

She swirled a sip of coffee in her mouth, and then took a

bite of her blueberry tart. The flakey crust tasted like ashes in her mouth. Worry for Nick knotted her insides.

He planned to deliver himself to De Luca along with the file proving he was the new-and-improved T.J. Paglietti. Once De Luca had T.J., or at least the man he thought was T.J., in his clutches, he'd order his female accomplice to take Miranda to a drop-off point where Lacey could pick her up.

Then what?

She dragged the fork tines through the melting ice cream and stabbed the top. Nick had convinced himself that Frankie De Luca was working alone and reassured Lacey he could take him on and escape. That might work if Nick had his trusty gun with him, but De Luca would search him. How could Nick, unarmed, defeat a man with a gun? And what if De Luca didn't believe Nick was T.J.?

A tremble rippled through her body, and she clicked her cup in the saucer, sloshing coffee over the side. Nick had refused to tell her where he was meeting De Luca. He warned her against calling the cops or the FBI and putting Miranda's life in danger.

She jumped up from the table and prowled back and forth across the sitting room, her helplessness like beating wings in her chest. She was lousy at doing nothing. Ever since Dad left the family, she'd been busy doing something—finding a new house for Mom and Ryan, hauling Ryan out of trouble, taking care of Mom during her illness.

Just because Nick offered a strong shoulder to lean on didn't mean she had to fall over once that shoulder disappeared. She'd find a way to help him.

She checked her watch. If she left now, she'd be forty-five minutes early to their meeting. She grabbed her jacket from the closet. More time to convince Nick to let this unfold a different way.

A light glowed from the front window of Nick's house as

Lacey pulled up to the curb. Peering into the dark yard, she swallowed and gripped the strap of her purse. She took a deep breath, pulling her shoulders back. She had nothing to fear from Frankie De Luca now. He had what he wanted.

And she had to get it back.

She swung open the gate and strode up the walkway toward the halo of light cast by the porch lamp. She stabbed the button for the doorbell and listened to its deep tone echo behind the front door.

Maybe Nick was in the shower. She had shown up early. She clicked open the screen door, and her heart flip-flopped. Someone had taped a white envelope to the door. She snatched it off and ripped it open. Her eyes skimmed the lines of the note, her throat tightening along with her grip on the paper.

Damn. Nick had left already. He'd scribbled out instructions for her to meet the eleven o'clock train at platform two of the Embarcadero BART station. Miranda would be on that train…alone.

He couldn't do this. He couldn't just leave her without a goodbye. What if he didn't make it back to her?

Shoving the note in her pocket, she lifted the heavy brass knocker, letting it fall once. Creeping to the edge of the porch, she leaned over to peak in the window, but the drapes obscured her view of the room.

Leaves crackled behind her and she spun around, prickles of fear dancing up her spine. A man stepped out of the shadows, a black knit cap pulled over his head. Crying out, she stepped back and lost her balance.

As she teetered on the edge of the porch, the man gripped her arm and yanked her forward. She opened her mouth for another scream when he pulled her closer and put his gloved finger to her lips.

"Shh, I'm T.J. Paglietti."

Chapter Fourteen

Lacey gulped back her scream. Chest to chest with the man claiming to be T.J., she could smell the spearmint of his gum and a heavy, musky cologne. Her gaze tracked across his rugged features, her terror mounting with every second.

This man didn't look a thing like Nick.

She jerked in his grasp and kicked his leg.

"Ouch, damn it. Is that any way to treat Dr. Marino's big brother?"

"You're not Nick's brother. You don't even resemble him."

He lifted a broad shoulder. "Can I help it if I got all the looks in the family? Don't forget, Florence Nightingale, Dr. B cut my face."

Her pulse fluttered, but she stopped struggling. It was useless, anyway. Judging from his dark outline, the man was built like a bull. "How do you know who I am? How do you even know Nick confided in me about…his brother?"

"I've been watching Nick."

"Who are you?"

"I told you. I'm T.J. 'Pretty Boy' Paglietti, Miranda's father, the guy who's gonna make sure Big Jimmy De Luca stays in the joint where he belongs."

With her free hand, Lacey rubbed her eye, shaking her head. "But you're supposed to have Nick's face now."

The face he did have creased, and he dropped her arm. "I don't know what you're talking about, sweetheart, but we can't stand out here all night yammering about my face. Let's go inside."

"We can't. Nick's not home and he has more security measures for this place than Fort Knox."

"But I don't have the alarm code and key to Fort Knox." He dangled a key chain from his finger, and she exhaled. He had to be Nick's brother.

He punched in a series of numbers on the keypad by the front door and slid the key into the lock. He pushed the door open, and they stepped into the foyer of the silent house.

She gasped and swung around to face him. "Miranda's been kidnapped."

"I know, and we're going to get her back tonight." His full lips formed a thin, hard line, the creases at the sides of his mouth deepening. "You need to tell me everything."

"You first. How do you know what's going on?"

"I told you. I've been doing a little reconnaissance ever since I heard Frankie De Luca planned to kill me before I could testify against his brother. I still have my sources. When Dr. B was murdered, I kept my distance from Nick because I didn't want anyone to connect us. I guess it didn't matter. Frankie discovered his identity, anyway."

"That's because Nick came to my rescue and insisted on protecting me. It raised a red flag, and Frankie got close to one of Nick's nurses to find out more about him."

She threw herself into a chair by the marble fireplace. "If he had just gone about his business after Dr. B was murdered, De Luca would've never connected him to you, and Miranda would be safe and your aunt wouldn't be in the hospital."

He perched on the chair across from her, swiping the knit cap from his head. Thick brown hair shot out in all directions. "I never really believed Frankie would go after a child. I hope Nick intends to give Frankie the goods on me in exchange for Miranda."

"Not exactly." She squeezed her hands between her knees. "He intends to exchange himself for Miranda."

T.J.'s brows shot up. "How's he going to do that? Frankie doesn't want Dominick Paglietti. He wants the other Paglietti brother."

Digging the heels of her hands into her eyes, she dragged in a ragged breath. "Nick's going to pose as you…and he has the documents to prove it."

"You have some explaining to do." He narrowed his blue eyes, his jaw tightening. Lacey suppressed a shiver, remembering she was in the presence of a hardened criminal.

She told T.J. about the before-and-after photos in Dr. B's file, and how the "after" photo was Nick's face. She waved her hand at him. "Did you look like Nick and then change your face again? I don't understand."

"That makes two of us." He frowned, sucking in his bottom lip. "A few months after Dr. B changed my face, he contacted me to let me know he'd kept my file with the before-and-after shots. He didn't ask for any more money at the time, but he implied he'd hold on to the file for future possibilities."

"Ugh. That's so horrible." She covered her face with her hands, feeling nauseous that she'd ever trusted or cared for Dr. B. "He must've blackmailed or threatened to blackmail the others, too, because yours wasn't the only file we found."

He shrugged his massive shoulders. "Those are the risks you live with."

"But those aren't Nick's risks. Why did Dr. B slip a photo

of Nick in that file? Did he even know you and Nick were brothers when he performed the surgery?"

"He knew. My bad. I couldn't resist bragging to Dr. B about my little brother, the hotshot plastic surgeon. I had no idea the doc would use that against me. He must've stuck Nick's picture in there to up the ante on the blackmail. It's one thing to threaten me with exposure, but he must've known I'd brave the fires of hell to protect my brother."

"The feeling is mutual. Nick's willing to risk everything he has to save your life and Miranda's."

"I'm not going to allow that to happen." T.J. pushed out of the chair, knocking it to the floor. "Do you know where he went to meet De Luca?"

"No, but he went early. He was supposed to meet me here first and give me the directions for collecting Miranda." She pulled the crumpled note from her pocket. "Instead he took off and left me this note."

T.J. held out his hand, and she dropped the note into it. He shook it out and read it quickly. "Chances are if Miranda's coming back to the Embarcadero station, Nick's going to leave from that station." He took a turn around the room. "Do you know where and how Nick got his instructions from De Luca?"

"Y-yes. De Luca called Nick's exchange and left a phony message about a face-lift, along with a phone number. Nick was home at the time and called him back from his cell."

"You were here with him?"

Two spots of heat dabbed Lacey's cheeks. Had T.J. figured out she and Nick were more than co-conspirators? "Yeah, I was here when he got and made the call."

"Look, I don't care if you're sleeping with my brother. Did he write the info down anywhere? Could he have left it here?"

She shook her head. "I doubt it. As soon as he wrote it down, he ripped it off the pad of paper."

"A pad of paper, huh?" T.J. stopped pacing. "Where's this pad of paper?"

"It's up in the bedroom." A zing of hope sizzled along her skin. Could Nick's pen have made an impression on the pages of the notepad? "Are you thinking what I think you're thinking?"

T.J. tapped his head. "Great minds think alike."

LOUNGING AGAINST THE cement post, Nick checked his watch. He'd wandered around the city for at least an hour. He had to throw Lacey off, didn't want to be there when she got to his place, didn't want to say goodbye. Didn't want to look in her eyes, knowing the goodbye might be forever.

He had to do this. The hunch that Frankie De Luca was working alone gave him hope. One on one, he could take Frankie, although adding a gun to the mix changed the playing field. He had his own gun tucked in his waistband beneath his jacket, but De Luca would relieve him of that in two seconds.

He had to save Miranda. If he could manage to get out of this in one piece, get back to Lacey, all the better. If not…

He hunched his shoulders against the brisk wind whipping through the station, tucking the leather satchel that contained Miranda's salvation under his arm. De Luca told him which train to take and to look for a dark blue sedan on the other end. He knew that car.

Once Nick revealed to De Luca that he was T.J. Paglietti and showed him the photos as proof, De Luca would send the woman with Miranda back onto the train. She'd look for Lacey, and then shove Miranda off the train, never getting off herself just in case Lacey showed up with the cops.

And then he'd be a dead man.

A smile twisted his lips. Funny, the one time in his life he had something…someone to live for, he had to give it all up.

The train's lights flashed down the tunnel, and he moved toward the track with the other passengers, every muscle taut with expectation.

A short ride later, Nick emerged from the station and ducked his head to avoid the pelting rain. He drew up the collar of his jacket and shoved his hands in the pockets, pressing the satchel against the side of his body. He walked briskly down the sidewalk toward the corner where a coffeehouse emitted warmth, laughter and the aroma of normalcy.

He could've had all that with Lacey, but as much as he wanted that life, he had debts to settle from his old life. If he could just save Miranda, T.J. and himself and return safely back to Lacey's arms.

Yeah, right. He performed superhuman feats in the operating room, but he was on his brother's turf now and felt more like a sidekick than a hero.

Folding his arms, he crushed the satchel against his chest as he wedged his back against the brick wall of the coffeehouse. A dark sedan crawled to a stop at the curb, the passenger window rolling down.

Frankie De Luca leaned across the seat. "Get in, Doc."

Nick slid into the car and snapped his seat belt into place, his gun digging into his gut. He jerked as a man, smelling of old cigarettes and booze, poked his head between the two front seats.

De Luca gestured back with his thumb. "Don't try nothin' funny, Doc. I got some backup here."

Damn. So much for Frankie working alone with a female accomplice. Nick bunched his hands into his arms.

He sure as hell wished *he* had some backup.

"NICK NEEDS ALL THE BACKUP he can get," Lacey hissed into her cell phone. "Do not cut me out, or I'll run squealing to the feds."

T.J. laughed. "And endanger Miranda? I don't think you'd do that, but I admire your moxie. Okay. I'm at the corner of Fifth and Garden, where a blue car just picked him up at the corner. Be here in thirty seconds, 'cuz I'm heading out on his tail…."

She swung open the car door of T.J.'s rental and dropped on the passenger seat, snapping her cell phone shut. "I stayed out of sight, but not too far away in case you tried to dump me."

Shaking his head, he said, "Keep low in the seat. If Frankie makes this car, I don't want him to see you."

Nick must've learned how to drive from his brother. T.J. took more twists and turns than a roller coaster, but they never lost sight of the blue car for long.

The car made a sharp turn onto a side street, and T.J. cruised past and double-backed through an alley just in time. The blue sedan pulled up in front of a nondescript tract house with a sagging white picket fence that matched every other house on the block of the working-class neighborhood.

T.J. reversed through the alley and parked on the street one block over from the house. He turned toward her and grabbed her shoulders. "Listen, we do this my way and hopefully no one gets hurt. Got it?"

She gulped and nodded. While in pursuit of De Luca and Nick, T.J. had noticed another person in the car with them— and it wasn't a woman. Here she was again, putting herself on the line for someone else. Would Nick leave her like all the others?

She'd tried to be a good daughter, so her father wouldn't leave the family, and he left, anyway, and started another family. She'd tried to be a good sister and keep Ryan out of trouble, and he repaid her by joining the military and putting himself in danger. She'd tried to be a good caretaker, but her mother had died.

Even Dr. B had betrayed her.

And Nick? How would he reward her selflessness?

"Are you ready to do this?"

They slipped out of the car and crept down the alley, keeping to the shadows, their shoes splashing in the occasional puddle. When they got to the street, T.J. took her hand and pulled her in the opposite direction of the house.

"We'll come up on it from behind. It's small, and it doesn't look like there are any basements in these houses."

They traipsed across a few backyards, incurring the wrath of a terrier trapped behind the gates of his dog run. T.J. growled back. "God, I hate dogs."

Landing in the backyard of the small house, Miranda's prison, they edged along the walls, checking each window. Sheets hung over each one, the gaps at the sides allowing them a peek into each room.

At the last window, Lacey pressed her face against the glass and gasped. She tugged at T.J.'s sleeve and pointed to the opening. He hunched down and peered through the window, and then fell back on his heels.

"Damn, they have Miranda in there."

"Is she all right?"

"Looks like she's sleeping." He held his hand out. "Wait, someone's coming into the room—Nick, Frankie—I can see two other sets of legs…a woman and another man."

She whispered, "What are we going to do?"

"They won't try anything with Miranda sleeping there. They better not. We'll wait until they leave the room. Maybe we can get Miranda to open this window and get in this way. I can tell you one thing—this ain't no mob hideaway. This is Frankie's party, and his alone. He doesn't have the backing of the family for this little venture."

The fact that one person called the shots instead of an

entire mob empire made the situation only slightly better. She may not be sleeping with the fishes tomorrow morning, but Miranda was in there, and Nick planned to let Frankie know he was his sworn enemy, T.J. Paglietti, the man standing next to her.

NICK CROUCHED NEXT TO Miranda, who was curled up on a mattress, and brushed a soft curl from her cheek. "Has she been upset, crying? What did you tell her?"

"I didn't tell her her father was a rat bastard and a stoolie." Frankie De Luca crossed his arms over his beefy chest, lodging a shoulder against the doorjamb. "Don't hand me any BS, Doc. I know she's T.J.'s kid. Why do you think I took her?"

Nick ignored the question. "The family doesn't know about this. Even the De Lucas wouldn't sanction taking a child."

"I told you, Frankie." The bleached blonde in the corner popped her gum through a scowl.

"Shut up, Tiff." Frankie's eyes darted from his woman to the low-life scum he had helping him out. A light sheen of sweat moistened Frankie's upper lip.

Nick tilted his chin toward Tiffany. "Has Miranda been okay?"

"She's a doll." The woman's overly made-up features softened as she looked at Miranda. "Don't worry. We plucked her from the car before sending it over the edge. She's been a little scared and confused, but after the accident we told her we had to take her because her aunt was hurt, and you had to take care of her aunt. She only cries sometimes."

Nick's gut twisted. He'd kill Frankie for that alone.

Too bad Frankie patted him down at the doorway and took his gun. If he could stall Frankie, he might be able to surprise him, knock the weapon out of his hand. Frankie's hapless cohort wouldn't prove much of a challenge. The guy appeared half drunk or high on something. Frankie probably paid him off with drugs. Tiffany wouldn't pose a problem, either. She had a soft spot for Miranda, and she wouldn't hurt her. Maybe he could even get her to help him.

Nick pushed up from the floor of the bedroom. "I'm thirsty. Can I get a beer or something?"

Frankie's eyes narrowed to slits. "What's the matter, not ready to hand over the goods on T.J. yet?"

"What do you think? You have a brother."

"Yeah, one who spent the past ten years in prison, thanks to your brother."

"T.J.'s been in his own prison for the past three years after you traded information with the feds to get his identity. I'd lay a ten-thousand-dollar bet in Vegas the family didn't know about your cooperation with the fibbies, either. Who'd you give up to them to get the goods on T.J.?"

The skin around Frankie's tight lips blanched. "Get him a beer, Tiff."

As he turned to follow Tiffany out of the bedroom, something caught Nick's eye at the window—a movement, a flash of jewelry. Then he saw Lacey's pale face pressed to the glass for a moment, and his hands fisted at his sides as he turned toward the door.

How had she done it? How had she found this place?

Frankie brought up the rear with his gun pointed at Nick's back. Nick clung to the doorjamb. "We need to shut this door. I don't want Miranda to hear anything."

Frankie glanced back and shrugged.

Nick wiped his brow with the back of his hand. A closed door would at least give Lacey a chance to carry out whatever madness she planned.

"THEY CLOSED THE DOOR. I think Nick saw me." Lacey whispered, "What now?" They'd already tried the window, but it was locked.

"We wake up Miranda and get her to open the window."

"You're crazy." Lacey brushed a drop of rain from the end of her nose. "She's a little girl."

"She's a Paglietti." T.J. tapped on the window while Lacey tugged on his arm, but a few minutes later the sheet bunched up and Miranda peeked through the window, rubbing sleepy eyes with her fist.

Lacey pressed her nose against the wet window and waved. Miranda's eyes widened, but she smiled and waved back. Placing her palms on the glass, Lacey moved them to the side. The plain, aluminum windows circa 1972 opened with a simple latch, sliding along a track.

Lacey jerked her thumb to the left. Would Miranda understand?

The little girl smiled and put a hand over her mouth. "She doesn't get it, T.J." She smiled back at Miranda, hiding her frustration.

Miranda leaned forward and blew a breath on the window. Then she wrote *hi,* even though the word was transposed for Lacey.

T.J. breathed in her ear. "Smart kid, huh? I knew I could count on Nick and my aunt Paula."

Lacey's pulse throbbed in her throat. She remembered Nick bragging that his niece could already read and write and wasn't even in kindergarten yet.

On the rain-streaked window, Lacey wrote *open* with the word and letters transposed so Miranda could read the message from her side. Miranda ran her hand across the word and smooshed her face against the window.

Lacey tapped on the word, now melting into rivulets of

water, and motioned to Miranda to open the window. Miranda flattened her palms against the glass as Lacey had done from the outside and pushed. Lacey pointed to the middle of the window frame where she suspected the latch might be.

Miranda's small hands scrambled at the side of the window while Lacey nodded. When she heard the click of the latch, she exhaled. Miranda pulled at the sliding window, and when a crack appeared, Lacey inserted her fingers and helped Miranda glide it open.

T.J. grinned. "I told you. She's a Paglietti through and through. You take Miranda back to the car, and I'll get Nick out of there."

"Come on, Miranda. Climb out." Lacey reached through the window, her hands skimming Miranda's shoulders as she backed up.

Miranda shook her head and stuck her thumb in her mouth.

Lacey pasted the smile on her face. "Come on, honey. You remember me, don't you?"

She popped her thumb out of her mouth. "Uncle Nick's here."

Glancing at T.J., she said, "She must've heard his voice when he was in the room." She turned back to the little girl, now an arm's length away. "I know your uncle Nick is here. He wants you to come with me now."

Miranda stepped farther away from the window into the room.

T.J. grunted. "She's a Paglietti, all right—stubborn to the core. I'll climb in there and hand her out to you. I gotta stick around, anyway, for some unfinished business."

WITH FRANKIE'S GUN POINTED at his head, Nick unzipped the satchel and drew out the file that would save his brother's life. Now he just had to work on saving his own.

"I'm finally going to get even with T.J. Paglietti for ratting out my brother, and I'll score some points with Pop." Frankie licked his lips.

Tiffany snorted. "Is he going to make you a captain now?"

"Shut up, Tiff." Frankie stuck out his free hand, palm upward, wiggling his fingers.

Nick slapped the file into Frankie's hand, sealing his fate. "T.J.'s new mug better be in here." He waved the file at Tiffany. "Do something useful for a change. Open this up, will ya?"

Snatching the folder from his hand, she said, "You never would've lasted two minutes with that little girl without me."

She flipped the file open with one long, manicured fingernail. "What am I looking for?"

"A before-and-after photo of T.J. It's in the back." Nick kept his eye on the gun leveled at him. When he saw the picture, would Frankie shoot first, ask questions later? Nick's jaw tensed.

"You remember what that punk, T.J., looked like, don't you?" Frankie's thin lips sneered, and he tightened his grip on the big .45.

"Mmm, of course I remember Pretty Boy. I just hope the surgery didn't ruin him." Tiffany shuffled through the papers and pulled out a photo. Her brows arched and her red collagen lips pursed into a rosebud. "I don't get it."

Frankie rolled his eyes. "It's simple—T.J. before, T.J. after. Let's see the picture so I can nail the bastard on his way into the courthouse to testify against Big Jimmy."

"It's him." Tiffany turned the photo around, pinching the corners between her blood-red acrylic nails. "It's the doc."

Snatching the picture from Tiffany's hand, Frankie swore as his forehead beaded with sweat. "What kind of trick are you trying to pull? Don't forget, I have the kid in there."

As if on cue, Miranda squealed from the bedroom. *Damn.*

Nick didn't want to go in there. This distraction couldn't have come at a worse time. Or maybe this was the perfect time.

Frankie's hand shook as he gestured Nick toward the bedroom door. "What the hell is going on? You first, Doc."

Lacey better be out of that room, and Miranda better be with her.

Nick shoved open the door, and his jaw dropped as Tiffany gasped behind him.

Miranda stood in the corner with her hands clapped over her mouth while half of Lacey's body hung into the room over the windowsill. But most surprising of all was the tall, vaguely familiar man in the center of it all, extending his hand to Miranda.

"Who the hell are you?" Frankie swung his weapon between the stranger, Lacey stuck in the window, and Nick. He yelled, "Get your ass in here, Teddy."

Teddy stumbled into the room, clutching his gun in one hand and a bottle of beer in the other. His mouth hung open, and a trickle of beer dribbled down his chin.

Perfect. Nick's muscles coiled.

Frankie shouted out orders, his voice hoarse. "Teddy, keep your eye on the doc. Tiffany, get the girl."

Teddy pointed an unsteady weapon at Nick while Tiffany ran across the room to grab Miranda's hand, but Miranda broke away from her and ran to Nick, clutching him around the legs. He reached down and smoothed her unruly hair.

Eyes wild, Frankie's gaze darted around the room, his plan falling apart in front of him. He settled on Lacey. "Get in this room, or I'll shoot your boyfriend right here and now."

Lacey scrambled over the edge and landed on the floor, her face flushed and her hair as wild as Miranda's. Nick's gut constricted. If Frankie laid another hand on Lacey, he'd kill him.

"Move over here next to the big guy." He pointed a finger

at the stranger planted in the middle of the room. "Now, who the hell are you?"

"Don't you recognize me, Frankie? I'm T.J. Paglietti."

Chapter Fifteen

The familiar voice settled on Nick's bones, and he grinned at
his brother. Leave it to T.J. to ride in like the calvary in a John
Wayne movie…and bring the girl with him. He sure as hell
better not have tried any of that Pretty Boy crap on Lacey.

Nick cleared his throat. "That's BS. You saw the before-
and-after. I'm T.J. Paglietti."

"C'mon, bro. You and your girlfriend take Miranda home
and me and Frankie will settle this mano a mano.

"Look, buddy, I don't know who the hell you are, cop,
fibbie, but I'll settle this with Frankie. Besides, you sound like
a bad imitation of a B gangster movie."

The gun trained on Nick trembled. "Sh-shut up, both of
you." Frankie waved the photo in front of him. "I have the
proof right here. He's T.J." He thrust his gun toward Nick.

Nick's hand tightened on Miranda's shoulder. "Miranda,
go over to Tiffany for a minute. We'll get out of here soon."

Miranda hung on to his leg but turned her head toward Tiffany.

"C'mon, honey. I'll get you a soda and a cupcake."

Nick nudged her back. Miranda didn't need soda and a
cupcake, but he didn't need Miranda in the line of fire. She
looked up at him, and he nodded. As she left the room with
Tiffany, he let out a long breath.

"Frankie, I see you don't have any more brains than you did ten years ago." T.J. laughed. "How does T.J. Paglietti become a world-famous plastic surgeon?"

Frankie blinked and the incriminating photo drifted to the floor. "Who said he was a world-famous plastic surgeon? He could've gone to medical school in those ten years, and besides, maybe he's a fake doctor."

"Frankie, Frankie, Frankie." T.J. shook his head. "What would your pop say?"

"Shut your mouth. My pop's gonna be happy when I kill…one of you and get Big Jimmy out of the slammer."

"And they say you're stupid, Frankie." Nick dug his heels into the carpet ready to do battle with his big brother. "Don't let this…fibbie fool you. I'm no world-famous plastic surgeon. I'm a fake, practicing without a license. Besides, this guy's too big to be T.J."

Frankie's gaze shifted to T.J. "He's right. Pretty Boy's lean, built more like the doc."

"Yeah, well, I've had a lot of free time on my hands, been lifting a lot of weights. You'll have that opportunity, too, Frankie, once you go to the big house. Might want to work on getting rid of that gut. Too much cannelloni?"

Frankie swung his gun back toward T.J. "I don't know which one of you is T.J. Paglietti, but I don't give a rat's ass anymore. I'm gonna whack both of you. Then maybe I'll kill the annoying nurse for good measure."

Nick's hands fisted. If Frankie touched Lacey, he'd tear the man apart with his bare hands.

"Which one should I take, boss?" The accomplice-for-hire with a fondness for booze waved his gun around the room.

T.J. snorted. "Your standards have really gone down, Frankie. Where'd you pick up this guy, the Mission District?"

"What's the matter, Big Daddy De Luca didn't loan you

any of his hit men for this job? Oh, that's right. He doesn't know a thing about it." Nick tightened his muscles into a coil, ready to spring into action.

His gaze, edged with a warning, flicked to Lacey, who looked carved from marble. Would she know enough to get down when the bullets started flying? Yeah, she'd learned a lot these past few weeks. Leave it to him to teach a woman how to dodge gunfire.

"You've been screwing up ever since you murdered Dr. Buonfoglio and his nurses, the very people who could've told you T.J. Paglietti was working right down the hall." Nick laughed. "Pretty good cover, huh?"

"I'm sick of both of you. Teddy, you take care of the doc. I'm gonna get rid of the muscle man." Frankie raised the gun level with T.J.'s head.

Nick bunched his hands into fists, rolling forward on the balls of his feet.

Time to settle his debt once and for all.

ICY FINGERS CLUTCHED at Lacey's heart as Nick lunged at Frankie, knocking his arm toward the ceiling. A shot went off, and the window to her left shattered. She dropped to the floor.

Tiffany screamed from the other room. Or was that her scream?

T.J. charged Teddy, who swung the gun around and aimed it at his chest. T.J. dived to the floor, trying to grab Teddy's legs.

Frankie struggled to bring the gun down, but Nick shoved his head into Frankie's armpit, forcing his arm up at an awkward angle. Frankie squeezed off another bullet, which hit the ceiling, raining plaster down onto everyone.

Teddy swore as T.J. yanked his legs out from under him. Gripping his gun with both hands as he fell, Teddy pointed at the grappling forms of Nick and Frankie.

"Nick, look out," Lacey screamed, a dreaded feeling of déjà vu smothering her.

Teddy squeezed the trigger just as Nick twisted Frankie's arm behind him and pushed him forward. Frankie took the impact of the bullet and slumped to the floor.

T.J. brought his booted foot down on Teddy's wrist, and Lacey's stomach turned as she heard it crack.

Lacey rose to her knees. Nick had Frankie's gun trained on Frankie, bleeding from the chest and ready to pass out. T.J. had Teddy's gun pointed at Teddy's head as he lay moaning on the threadbare carpet, holding his wrist and rocking back and forth.

Tiffany burst into the room, stopping short at the threshold. She shoved Miranda behind her, and then held up her hands. "I don't want any trouble, boys. Frankie forced me to stay here and watch Miranda."

T.J. looked up. "You tell the cops what went down here, or our version of it, and we'll let them decide what to do with you. In fact, why don't *you* call 911 to make it look good?"

As Tiffany retreated to the other room to make the call, Miranda darted toward Nick and grabbed his leg. He hoisted her onto his hip and reached down to pull Lacey up, bringing her into the curve of his arm. He kissed the side of her head, and that's all she needed, all she wanted. She'd never felt safer in her life, and it had nothing to do with the two men vanquished on the floor.

Nick nuzzled her ear. "I tried to keep you out of it, the last act of this freak show I call a life, but you just kept coming back for more."

"Did you think I'd scare off that easily?" She nestled in close to his body and stroked Miranda's hair. "I've made a career out of helping those in need."

"Speaking of those in need, it looks like Frankie needs a doctor." T.J. prodded an unconscious Frankie with his foot.

"I just forgot the Hippocratic Oath. Let the paramedics handle him. How about you? Are you okay, bro?"

"Me?" T.J. pocketed Teddy's gun and shoved him into a corner with his foot. "You're the one who made the first move. Surprised the hell out of me, but you saved my life. Are you satisfied now? Will you stop with the crazy idea you owe me something?"

"You're right. Maybe I owe myself something."

Lacey's heart thrummed against Nick's chest as he squeezed her tighter. Maybe she owed herself the same something.

"Damn straight." T.J. grinned. "Take Miranda and Lacey in the other room. I'll keep an eye on these two until the cops and ambulance arrive."

"You're sticking around for the cops?" Lacey raised an eyebrow.

T.J. nodded. "This is self-defense, and I'm a very important government witness with some very important testimony to deliver day after tomorrow."

Nick hitched Miranda farther up on his hip and crouched down to sweep his picture from the floor. Rising, he crumpled the photo in his fist and shoved it into the pocket of his jacket. Grabbing Lacey's hand, he headed for the door.

She laced her fingers through his and rested her cheek against his shoulder. Nick was finally free of the debt that had pressed on him for twenty years.

NICK GRIPPED HIS BROTHER'S hand, and T.J. pulled him into a brief hug. "You sure you wouldn't rather come back to my place, start getting to know your daughter?"

"Nothing I'd rather do, but I have to go with the cops. Me and my girl will have lots of time to catch up." He punched Nick's shoulder as if to make up for his moment of brotherly affection. "Chu promised me protective custody until I testify and a phone call to my attorney. I'll be okay. Miranda's still a little wobbly. There's time enough for me and Cee Cee to reacquaint ourselves with her."

T.J. tossed him the keys to his car before he followed the police officer to the squad car.

Nick swallowed. T.J.'s words carved a hole in his heart. He knew he'd have to give Miranda back to her parents one day. He just didn't realize how hard it was going to be.

Then a pair of arms wrapped around his waist and Lacey rested her head on his back, and that hole started healing. He turned and embraced her. "Are you all right?"

"I am now even if it's just for this moment."

"Don't you expect we'll have more moments like this?"

She stifled a sob. "I've learned not to expect much from the people I love, except their desertion."

He tipped her chin up and kissed a tear from her cheek. "Do you really believe I'd desert you now? You're the only woman who knows me and all my imperfections. The only woman I've ever let get close enough to see those imperfections. And you're still here."

"I'm not going anywhere." She caressed his face with her hands. "And you're still Dr. Perfect to me."

"Dr. Marino?" Detective Chu strode toward them. "The EMTs checked out your niece, and she's fine. You can take her home now."

"Thanks, Detective."

"Funny how Frankie De Luca was after your brother all this time, and you didn't even realize it." Chu unwrapped a piece of hard candy and popped it in his mouth.

"Yeah, what a coincidence I moved into the same building and on the same floor as the doctor who changed my brother's face." Nick clutched the leather satchel to his chest.

"Lots of coincidences." Chu clicked the candy in his

mouth as his gaze dropped to the satchel. "Your brother contacts you just when your niece is kidnapped. You and Ms. Kirk together again?"

"Ms. Kirk's my fiancée. It's natural we'd be together when I got my brother's call." He draped an arm around Lacey's shoulder, pinching her.

"Well, congratulations all around, then."

Lacey wriggled away from Nick's protective arm and dug into her pocket. "One more thing, Detective Chu." She opened her hand, and a small silver key winked in the dark. "I remembered this key just last night. Dr. Buonfoglio gave it to me a while back for safekeeping. He told me it opened a wall safe in his daughter's closet, the one who lives in the group home in Santa Cruz."

Detective Chu pinched the key between two fingers as he took it from her palm. "Maybe that's what De Luca was after all along. Just remembered it, huh?"

"Completely slipped my mind before."

"Anything taken out of that safe recently?"

"Not that I know of." Lacey sidled next to Nick, and he curled an arm around her waist, yanking her hip to hip.

"We want to get Miranda home, Detective. It's been a long night."

"You do that, Doc." Chu sauntered back to his unmarked car, tossing the key up in the air and whistling.

Lacey sagged against his body. "Do you think he knows?"

"Yeah, he knows."

She sighed. "Guess you better get Miranda home."

"Guess I better get both of you home." He cupped her face with one hand and ran a thumb across her luscious lips.

"You can stop with the undercover-lover stuff, Nick."

"Didn't you just tell me you wouldn't leave me?"

"For the here and now." Her bottom lip trembled, and she

caught it between her teeth. "You can drop the whole charade about my being your fiancée."

"I'm not talking about the here and now, Lacey. I'm talking about the forever and ever. And the fiancée part? That's only a charade if you say no."

"Say no?" Her silky lashes dropped over her eyes.

"In the past few weeks, you haven't shown a coy bone in your body, Lacey Kirk. Are you going to start batting those long lashes at me now?"

A man cleared his throat behind Nick, and he spun around. An EMT had Miranda by the hand. "She's good to go, Dr. Marino."

Miranda hurled herself into his arms, and he scooped her up. "Come on, ladies, time to go home."

Epilogue

Three days later, Lacey cuddled next to Nick on his sofa while the eleven o'clock news glowed from the TV in the corner.

Nick's aunt Paula had come out of her coma that morning. They told her they'd found and rescued Miranda, and her recovery looked like a sure thing.

Miranda slept soundly upstairs, most likely dreaming of her mother, who tomorrow planned to see her daughter for the first time in three years.

"Here's the story." Nick pointed the remote at the TV and raised the volume.

T.J., looking suave in his designer suit, posed on the top step of the courthouse with a sleek brunette at his side while cameras clicked and reporters shoved microphones in his face.

"You're right. Miranda looks just like her mom." She rubbed Nick's knuckles as his hand rested on her thigh.

The FBI had already gone after the agents T.J. accused of working with the De Lucas. The government knew they owed T.J. and were prepared to set him up with a new life...with his family.

More than anything, Nick wanted to make his brother whole, give him back the life T.J. sacrificed when he saved his younger brother from a couple of thugs and then took a job from the mob to avenge his family. But losing Miranda was going to hurt.

Could she make that hurt go away? Was her love enough? It had never been enough for anyone else.

"I know you're going to miss her, Nick." She brought his hand to her lips and kissed each knuckle.

With his other hand, Nick pressed the mute button and tossed the remote on the cushion. "I am, but she belongs with her mother and father. They can keep her safe now. I know she didn't recognize T.J. the other night, but she'll know her mother. She never stopped asking for Cee Cee."

"Are you going to be okay? Is there anything I can do?"

"You can answer that question we left hanging in the air before we collected Miranda and took her home."

Her fingertips buzzed with excitement, and her pulse hummed. "It wasn't exactly a question."

"You're a hard woman to please, Lacey." He dropped to one knee beside her. "Will you marry me? I think Miranda needs some cousins."

"You're asking me to become Mrs. Perfect?" She brushed a dark lock of hair from his forehead and traced her fingers over the planes of his face.

He captured her hands, kissing the insides of her wrist. "Don't expect perfection from me. I'm secretive by nature. I can slip on a mask faster than you can step into a pair of shoes. But I need you beside me to become the man behind this face. I'll never leave you, Lacey, and you don't have to do a thing to make me stay except love me."

She could do that.

He pulled her into a kiss that melted her last reservations. She could love him for a lifetime.

* * * * *

The Colton family is back!
Enjoy a sneak preview of
COLTON'S SECRET SERVICE by Marie Ferrarella,
part of THE COLTONS: FAMILY FIRST *miniseries.*

Available from Silhouette Romantic Suspense
in September 2008.

He cautioned himself to be leery. He was human and he'd been conned before. But never by anyone nearly so attractive. Never by anyone he'd felt so attracted to.

In her defense, Nick supposed that Georgie could actually be telling him the truth. That she was a victim in all this. He had his people back in California checking her out, to make sure she was who she said she was and had, as she claimed, not even been near a computer but on the road these last few months that the threats had been made.

In the meantime, he was doing his own checking out. Up close and exceedingly personal. So personal he could feel his blood stirring.

It had been a long time since he'd thought of himself as anything other than a law enforcement agent of one type or other. But Georgeann Grady made him remember that beneath the oaths he had taken and his devotion to duty, there beat the heart of a man.

A man who'd been far too long without the touch of a woman.

He watched as the light from the fireplace caressed the outline of Georgie's small, trim, jean-clad body as she moved about the rustic living room that could have easily come off the set of a Hollywood Western. Except that it was genuine.

As genuine as she claimed to be?

Something inside of him hoped so.

He wasn't supposed to be taking sides. His only interest in being here was to guarantee Senator Joe Colton's safety as the latter continued to make his bid for the presidency. Everything else was supposed to be secondary, but, Nick had to silently admit, that was just a wee bit hard to remember right now.

Earlier, before she'd put her precocious handful of a daughter to bed, Georgie had fed his appetite by whipping up some kind of a delicious concoction out of the vegetables she'd pulled from her garden. Vegetables that, by all rights, should have been withered and dried. She'd mentioned that a friend came by on occasion to weed and tend it. Still, it surprised him that somehow she'd managed to make something mouthwatering out of it.

Almost as mouthwatering as she looked to him right at this moment.

Again, he was reminded of the appetite that hadn't been fed, hadn't been satisfied.

And wasn't going to be, Nick sternly told himself. At least not now. Maybe later, when things took on a more definite shape and all the questions in his head were answered to his satisfaction, there would be time to explore this feeling. This woman. But not now.

Damn it.

"Sorry about the lack of light," Georgie said, breaking into his train of thought as she turned around to face him. If she noticed the way he was looking at her, she gave no indication. "But I don't see a point in paying for electricity if I'm not going to be here. Besides, Emmie really enjoys camping out. She likes roughing it."

"And you?" Nick asked, moving closer to her, so close that a whisper would have trouble fitting in. "What do you like?"

The very breath stopped in Georgie's throat as she looked up at him.

"I think you've got a fair shot of guessing that one," she told him softly.

* * * * *

*Be sure to look for COLTON'S SECRET SERVICE
and the other following titles from*
THE COLTONS: FAMILY FIRST *miniseries:*
RANCHER'S REDEMPTION by Beth Cornelison
THE SHERIFF'S AMNESIAC BRIDE by Linda Conrad
SOLDIER'S SECRET CHILD by Caridad Piñeiro
BABY'S WATCH by Justine Davis
A HERO OF HER OWN by Carla Cassidy

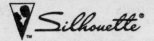

Silhouette®

Romantic
SUSPENSE

**Sparked by Danger,
Fueled by Passion.**

The Coltons Are Back!

Marie Ferrarella
Colton's Secret Service

The Coltons: Family First

On a mission to protect a senator, Secret Service agent
Nick Sheffield tracks down a threatening message only
to discover Georgie Gradie Colton, a rodeo-riding single
mom, who insists on her innocence. Nick is instantly
taken with the feisty redhead, but vows not to let his
feelings interfere with his mission. Now he must figure
out if this woman is conning him or if he can trust her
and the passion they share….

Available September wherever books are sold.

**Look for upcoming Colton titles
from Silhouette Romantic Suspense:**

RANCHER'S REDEMPTION by Beth Cornelison, Available October
THE SHERIFF'S AMNESIAC BRIDE by Linda Conrad, Available November
SOLDIER'S SECRET CHILD by Caridad Piñeiro, Available December
BABY'S WATCH by Justine Davis, Available January 2009
A HERO OF HER OWN by Carla Cassidy, Available February 2009

Visit Silhouette Books at www.eHarlequin.com SRS27598

6 HEROES. 6 STORIES.
ONE MONTH TO READ THEM ALL.

Harlequin Intrigue is dedicating
the month of September to those
heroes among men. Courageous
police, sexy spies, brave bodyguards—
they are all Intrigue's Ultimate Heroes.

In September, collect all 6.

Silhouette
Desire

Gifts from a Billionaire

JOAN HOHL

THE M.D.'S MISTRESS

Dr. Rebecca Jameson collapses from
exhaustion while working at a remote
African hospital. Fellow doctor Seth Andrews
ships her back to America so she can heal.
Rebecca is finally with the sexy surgeon
she's always loved. But would their affair
last longer than the week?

**Available September
wherever books are sold.**

Always Powerful, Passionate and Provocative.

Inside ROMANCE

Stay up-to-date on all your romance reading news!

The Inside Romance newsletter is a FREE quarterly newsletter highlighting our upcoming series releases and promotions!

Click on the <u>Inside Romance</u> link on the front page of **www.eHarlequin.com** or e-mail us at insideromance@harlequin.ca to sign up to receive your FREE newsletter today!

You can also subscribe by writing us at: HARLEQUIN BOOKS Attention: Customer Service Department P.O. Box 9057, Buffalo, NY 14269-9057

Please allow 4-6 weeks for delivery of the first issue by mail.

HARLEQUIN®

INTRIGUE®

COMING NEXT MONTH

INTRIGUE'S
ULTIMATE
HEROES
★

#1083 MONTANA ROYALTY by B.J. Daniels
Whitehorse, Montana
Devlin Barrow wasn't like any cowboy Rory Buchanan had ever rode with. The European stud brought status to her ranch—as well as a trail of assassins and royal intrigue.

#1084 BODYGUARD TO THE BRIDE by Dani Sinclair
Xavier Drake had been on difficult missions before, but none more challenging than posing as Zoe Linden's bodyguard. Once he got his hands on the pregnant bride, it would be tough giving her away.

#1085 SHEIK PROTECTOR by Dana Marton
Karim Abdullah was the most honorable sheik and the fiercest warrior throughout the desert kingdom. On his word he vowed to protect Julia Gardner and her unborn child—the future prince of his war-torn land.

#1086 SOLVING THE MYSTERIOUS STRANGER
by Mallory Kane
The Curse of Raven's Cliff
The fortune told of a dark and mysterious stranger who had the power to save Raven's Cliff. But could Cole Robinson do it without sacrificing the town's favorite daughter, Amelia Hopkins?

#1087 SECRET AGENT, SECRET FATHER by Donna Young
Jacob Lomax awoke with no memory and an overpowering instinct for survival. In a race against time, the secret agent had to reconstruct the last twenty-four hours of his life, if he was to save Grace Renne and the unborn child that may be his.

#1088 COWBOY ALIBI by Paula Graves
Tough, embittered Wyoming police chief Joe Garrison had one goal: finding the person responsible for his brother's murder. But when a beautiful amnesiac Jane Doe surfaced in need of his help, his quest for justice turned into the fight of their lives.